To Tin

with t.

splendid spring sojourn!

Murder in Antarctica

A Hieronymus Pound Mystery

George Quin

a. k. a. Ricardo

May 2023

Cover by Richard Guise

(Photo: Anvers Island, Antarctica)

Published by Richard Guise

Printed by Kindle Direct Publishing

ISBN: 9798393431020

Most of the locations used in this book are real. With the exception of some historical figures, all the characters are entirely fictitious.

The first question that nudged into his waking mind was how he could possibly have been asleep in this cold.
The second why could he see the sunset.
The third why his bed felt like ice.

Slowly squeezing through the numbness came answers.
It hadn't been a normal sleep.
It was sun*rise*.

And it *was* ice.

PART ONE   ESCAPE

PART TWO   CONTACT

PART THREE   CRISIS

PART FOUR   RETURN

PART

ONE

ESCAPE

1

Buenos Aires, February, morning

'Clemente!'

The smallest man in a tight knot of four glanced up before returning his gaze to the dusty summer gravel of the Plaza de Mayo. His short dark hair was cut with fashionable precision, stubble exactly three days old and the collar of his denim jacket carefully raised against an imaginary breeze. Two of the others were younger and more formally dressed, the other much older, his creased jacket hanging loosely from muscular shoulders.

It had been just a glance. The first time he'd heard the name since he left Spain. Off guard. Not now.

'Clemente! It's you, isn't it?' The caller, a tall man waving a tourist map, spoke in Spanish but with a Madrileño accent easy to spot here in Buenos Aires.

Training, thought the small man. Snap to it. Acting, it's what you do. Be the man you're supposed to be. *Be* him.

With the caller only three strides away, the small man spun his wiry frame around. Apart from a little gesture invisible to the rest of the group, he was every inch the bemused local.

'Me?' he said, voice steady. 'I think you've mistaken me for someone else.'

The caller was about to contradict him when he noticed the small man's right forefinger, held low before his belt and making the universal sign for 'No', before forming a cross with his left forefinger. This and the panic radiating from the small man's eyes brought the caller to a halt.

'Ah, yes. Sorry, señor,' he said and turned away. The small man let out the tiniest of sighs before flicking on a smile to face the group.

'Funny,' he said, 'I'm usually mistaken for Luís Suárez.' The brief cloud of tension that had hung over them was gone.

'Ha, it's the teeth, Javi,' said one of the well-dressed men, making the other laugh – but not the older man, whose eyes remained fixed on Javi. The small man's real name, though, was not Javier Lores, but Clemente Gil. And the tourist who'd recognised him was a fellow student at Gil's college back in Ávila six years before. Police college.

*

As the tourist rejoined his own group, the four men walked steadily to the edge of the square, their backs to the Casa Rosada and the balcony from which, before any of them were born, Eva Perón had addressed an adoring crowd. Turning first along Reconquista and then down streets of gradually less grandeur, the older man eventually led them through an unmarked door, down a single flight of steps and into a small, poorly lit bar whose only occupant was the barman. During this short stroll, though Gil heard himself making small talk with one of the well-dressed newcomers, his mind raced through a torrent of newly flowing issues. Though the Plaza de Mayo was well-known enough for anyone new to the city to find it, he'd thought it the wrong place to meet clients, but had kept his mouth shut. Too late now. Had Pepe realised the tourist really did know him? He was already acutely aware his stab at the answer would determine the next few years of his life – if he got them. Not sure. Training. No immediate threat, so carry on as normal. Make a rational assessment. If the answer is then yes, send the pre-arranged message at the earliest opportunity.

Carry on as normal? What did 'normal' mean in this world he'd fallen into? Fallen – who was he kidding? Carry on as what passes for normal in a drug-crazed world. Make the arrangements Javi would make. It's what you do. Arrangements he knew would not be fulfilled. Gil was familiar with his role in the meeting, or rather Javi's role. Pepe – no one ever used a surname, Gil never asked – would talk money, while he would talk logistics, after he'd ordered drinks for the clients. Even that early in the morning he'd kill for a beer. He took water.

The meeting was short, to the point and entirely predictable. Having spent over a year pushing Officer Clemente Gil to the furthest recess of his mind, he'd now resumed the thought-split he'd trained for: one set for Javi Lores and one for Clemente Gil. Javi's time frame was 48 hours and for this he made notes, checked times, chose places and looked to Pepe for confirmation. Gil's horizon was shorter. Much shorter. For this, he pictured the Subte, Buenos Aires' metro system, recalled bus routes, estimated times. Most of all, he cast his mind's eye around his apartment. Was it worth the risk?

The meeting finished, the four men shook hands and left the bar in two pairs. As Pepe and Javi walked back upstairs to the daylight, the sounds of the city gradually embracing them, Pepe turned to his junior partner.

'Everything OK, Javi?' he asked.

Javi kept his eyes on the stairs and his voice steady. 'Yep, all OK. I'm on it right away.'

'Back to Barracas?'

'Back to Barracas.'

*

One hour later, jacket collar still raised and now with a small khaki rucksack slung over one shoulder, Gil avoided eye contact with the other passengers as he boarded a bus out of the city. Tired as he suddenly was, he was still on full alert.

The hour's activities had been decisive and brisk. First, on the Subte, still stifling in late summer, he'd completed his assessment: yes, Pepe was probably on his case right now. Conclusion: get as far away from BA as he could, as fast as he could. No drugs would be supplied on schedule, no more drugs would be supplied via Javi Lores at all. That at least lifted a burden from Gil's shoulders. Standing in the train between Independencia and Constitución, pressed in by passengers, he'd tapped the message into his phone:

K. Sebastian. 02.00. J

Some things, life-critical things, are on fast recall. The saints' names chosen as code included Sebastian for 'cover blown'. '02.00' meant he didn't need instructions immediately, but would contact K again in about two hours. The identity of K, his local handler, Gil didn't know and didn't want to know. Checking the text carefully, he drew a long breath – ignoring for once the odour of his fellow passengers – and tapped Send.

Another weight lifted. He was on his way out. An image sprang unbidden to his mind – of his mother sitting on the sea wall somewhere in Andalucía while Clemente and his brother played on the sand – before he forced it out again.

The next decision had been made before stepping out onto the platform at Constitución. Yes, he must call at the apartment where his old passport and some cash were stashed, even though by now one of Pepe's associates would probably be loafing about nearby ready to report back: was Javi on or off the job?

The cocaine that reached Europe from Argentina didn't originate there, but came mostly from Peru or Bolivia. These countries, along with Paraguay, also supplied the greater part of the immigrants forming not just a pool from which dealers like Pepe could recruit his 'associates' but also, conveniently, some local customers. Most lived in the *villas*, BA's slums that the tourists, if they noticed them at all, would have seen only on their way in from the airport. One of these, known as Villa 21, was located in the district of Barracas and from this came the name by which Pepe's network was known: Grupo 21. Known not only among dealers but also to the city's anti-drugs agency. Knowing its name was one thing; knowing its sources, its routes, its clients, its personnel – that was quite another, and one where the surprising gift of a foreign recruit, unrecognised by any and willing to go undercover, was more than welcome. After an immersive six months for him to learn the city inside out, the agency had placed Gil in a suitably seedy one-bed apartment on the edge of Barracas, supplied him with one or two likely contacts and let him loose. A year, they'd reckoned – or sooner if he needed to get out. Minimum contact. Just to deliver intelligence or raise the alarm. By now, nine months in, the supply side of Grupo 21's activities, which is what – as Javier Lores – Gil had managed to get involved in, were almost as well understood by a small section of the BA police as by the dealers themselves. As soon as Gil moved out, they'd move in.

Calling at the apartment first could safely be interpreted as 'on the job'. Walking back out, complete with rucksack, may have been. Wandering north, away from Barracas, probably wouldn't. That's if he was being tailed at all. Gil didn't know and didn't look. Training: don't scan around, behave as normal, but plan your movements carefully. His careful route had brought Gil to the busy bus stop where he was avoiding eye contact with the queue as it boarded. Plenty had joined behind him. Eventually, almost full, the bus pulled into the stream of southbound traffic. Its destination board read 'Aeropuerto – Ezeiza'.

As it pulled into the next stop, Gil closed his eyes: don't fill up, don't fill up. Only two passengers boarded, leaving a few seats still vacant. He exhaled slowly: the driver was now bound to call at the following stop as well. Here, Gil left it to the last moment before getting off. As he did so, he casually turned his head – apparently to look at the sky but really to notice that a clutch of other late alighters from the rear of the bus had followed him: seven, he thought. One other bus was waiting and Gil immediately boarded it. Most of the others followed him. Yes, five of them. The bald guy with the big glasses. The tall man with the puffer jacket – didn't take it off even in the hot bus. A student-type in a Fidel Castro cap. An American guy with a huge case. And an overweight woman with a long green scarf that would probably catch in her wheelie-case. Maybe the last two were together.

Even before they were all seated, the bus departed northbound, its destination board reading 'Aeroparque – Jorge Newbery'. While Ezeiza was the international airport, Jorge Newbery handled most of Buenos Aires' domestic flights.

*

Had any of these five boarded the flight to Ushuaia? This was Gil's next question two hours later.

Knowing first hand that Grupo 21 had an extensive network around BA, he'd avoided the temptation of simply finding the earliest flight to Spain – there seemed little doubt that Pepe's contacts, possibly even customers, included some border personnel – and instead managed to make a phone booking on the first flight he could find to a distant enough destination inside Argentina. And you couldn't get more distant than Ushuaia, the growing Patagonian outpost on the southern shores of Tierra del Fuego. At least, thought Gil, it was still summer. Theoretically.

Of course, any tail outside the apartment could have followed just to the bus before handing over by phone to another at either airport. But anyway, at the gate and in the aircraft before taking his seat, Gil looked around as casually as he could for any among the five. Yes, there was the bald guy with the big glasses down at the front. Also in the queue was the tall man with the puffer jacket, but Gil didn't see where he sat. That was all. Sitting down in his aisle seat – not ideal, too exposed – he pushed his holdall down between his legs and then, knuckles interlocked, pretended to pray.

Yes, he told himself, pretence is what it was. Had he left Spain a believer? Maybe. And here in Argentina? If he, Clemente Gil, was doing good deeds – and as an undercover cop trying stop the flow of drugs surely he was – why would God desert him and place that idiot from police college in the same place at the same time? Gil expelled a derisory laugh before pulling himself straight. No, don't draw attention to yourself. Concentrate. You're still not Clemente, not till you get back to Spain, back to mama's house. Even after a dozen years away, that was still home. Hunching his short frame further below the headrest, he mouthed to himself: stay disciplined, invisible, discreet.

As he flicked through the in-flight magazine, the plane set off down the runway. With perfumes and whiskeys flashing past his eyes, he felt the aircraft lurch into the sky and the magazine fall from his hands. Bending into the aisle to retrieve it, his eyes met those of the young woman opposite.

'Nervous flyer?' she asked. Short blonde hair and leather jacket put the woman in her twenties, but something in the look Gil caught put her ten years older.

'Me? No,' he said, picking it up. 'I must have dropped off.'

'May I?' she asked, gesturing at the magazine. 'I don't seem to have one.'

'Of course,' said Gil. 'Too expensive for me anyway.'

They exchanged a smile before returning to their own thoughts. Concentrate, repeated Gil to himself. The other passengers. You've got nearly three hours before Ushuaia to spot the tail – if there is one. Come on, what did the training have on picking out a tail from more than one possibility? Does one of them keep reading the same paper? Hm, that was way out of date: does one keep glancing at their phone? Who reads papers these days? Wait – the tall guy in the puffer jacket had been doing exactly that every time Gil saw him. Where was he?

With the seat belt lights already out, Gil got to his feet and chose the longest walk to the toilets. Just three rows down he spotted the back of the tall man's head, puffer jacket on his lap – why not in the rack? – and walked past. On the way back, he caught the man's eyes and got back a hard, fixed stare. Without breaking stride, Gil recovered his seat. Must be him. Weapon in coat? Security at the Aeroparque had been slack. Domestic flight. Hadn't he seen that face at Pepe's house...?

*

Shuffling through Ushuaia's stylish, glass-and-wood terminal, some passengers shivered as they glanced out at the steel-grey sky above the peaks closing off the frontier town from the rest of the island, from the rest of the world. Back in Buenos Aires the cloak of dusk would soon descend on the capital but here in the far south the thin daylight still had hours to run. Most had probably been here before, thought Gil, probably lived here. He'd spent much of the flight trying to imagine Pepe's instructions. The boss would have assumed Group 21, his own careful creation, was already compromised and would be closing it down, while fixing Javi in the cross-hairs of a new operation. A much shorter operation. Nothing to be gained by simply tailing Javi all the way to his would-be escape. The instruction would be to deliver a revenge. A swift revenge.

With minimal checks once again, the passengers soon filed out of the cocoon of the terminal and into a blast of bitter Patagonian air. With no overcoat, Gil hunched his shoulders and looked around. High wire fences, storage facilities, scrubby vegetation. What a bleak place to die. No, he'd get through this. Training. Assume the worst, envisage the best. The tail would be somewhere behind. Stay in the crowd. They're dispersing – meet and greet, taxis, buses... One of the buses was clearly the shuttle into town and this Gil boarded. Safety in numbers. Such was the crush there was no opportunity to look for the tall man.

Though in recent years government support for settlement in the region had seen Ushuaia growing rapidly, the suburbs had nowhere to go but laterally along the coast of the Beagle Channel. The journey from the airport, located on a short peninsula jutting out into the channel, to the centre of town was therefore a short one and Gil soon found himself descending with most of the busload into the bustle of early-evening shoppers on Avenída San Martín, a surprisingly normal main street sheltered one block back from the seafront. Out of the corner of his eye Gil half-spotted one passenger taller than the rest in the line behind him. Without anything approaching a practical plan other than his new mantra – safety in numbers – he followed a clutch of men heading straight for the nearest bar, a well-lit building and clearly one of the few older, frontier-style structures that had survived. On one side a sign read 'Bar Ideal', which indeed it seemed to be. On the other, in jaunty lettering and in English to attract the tourists, another read 'The Bar at the End of the World'. Keeping his head well down and hoping the end of his own was still a long way off, Gil entered.

Inadvertently he'd let the door close on someone behind and, hearing a small cry, pulled it open again to see before him the short blonde woman from across the aeroplane's aisle.

'Sorry...' said Gil. '...oh, it's you.'

By way of reply she rubbed her nose before emitting a wince.

'Oh, you're hurt,' he continued. 'Please, let me find you a seat.'

The bar was busy with locals relaxing on their way home and tourists inspecting the photos and posters that crammed the walls. Gil noticed a table for two being vacated in the far corner and led the injured party in that direction before helping her carefully into a seat below a blue and white poster showing a map of two islands above the words '*Las Malvinas son Argentinas*'. Already the encounter had brought a sudden rush of normality to Gil – and a blast of common sense as bracing as the Patagonian air. Of course, he thought, the number that's safest is two.

'Are you all right?' he asked, still standing.

'I don't think it's broken,' she said, gingerly touching the bridge of her nose. Her accent was vaguely Argentinian but with a strange twang.

'It was clumsy of me. My mind was elsewhere. I'm sorry. Can I get you a drink?'

'It is I that should buy you a drink.'

'Why?'

'Because this is my town and I think you're new here. I should welcome you.'

As she began to empty her bag in search of a purse, he laughed – actually laughed for the first time since his Luís Suárez remark that morning – a morning that already seemed half a lifetime ago.

'No, no. It's the least I can do.'

'OK. A small beer, thanks.'

'Deal,' he said. 'I'll just pay a visit before getting us two beers.'

As he stepped away she called after him.

'My name's María,' she said.

'Clemente,' he said, exchanging a smile before turning away again.

Descending the steep stairs to the toilets, Gil bit his lips. He'd said it without thinking. Off guard. Probably nobody heard – and everyone around had already been in the bar anyway. Looking in the mirror in the gents, he saw a ragged and tired face staring back and found himself wondering how old his new friend was. There'd been something that caught his attention as she was emptying her bag. It wasn't until he was waiting at the bottom of the stairs while the sound of descending footsteps got nearer that he remembered what it was. The moment before he saw it.

Her blonde locks were hidden once again under the Fidel Castro cap. Many things merged into one moment. Eyes meeting. Gun rising. Cigarette machine crashing. Bullet pinging. Crack echoing. Two bodies tumbling.

First to his feet, Gil saw the weapon still in her hand and scrambled back down the corridor. Left, right. Sound of running behind. A door. There must be a door. There. Bar pushed. Steps up. Door opening behind. Gate or wall? Another loud crack. A short curse. Wall. He was over in an instant. Up hill or down? He was fitter than her. Up a steep street. Long steps for pavement. Long strides, short breaths, heart racing. Left. Street now level. Easier, faster. Right, harder. Left again, steady. Garden wall. Over in one. No lights in house. Shed locked. Crouching behind. Darkness. The sound of his own breathing, his own heart beating against his jacket. Slower. Slower...

Silence. A silence into which Gil's thoughts began to seep. If there'd been any lingering doubt that his cover really was blown, they'd been blasted away in a dank cellar at the end of the world. He'd fallen for the second oldest trick in the book: Pepe had known he'd be looking for a man on his tail, and so he'd sent a girl. If she hadn't taken the first opportunity of the two of them being out of sight together, he might have fallen for the oldest trick as well.

Clenching his fists at his own idiocy, Gil suddenly remembered his backpack, lifted one hand to his shoulder and let out a long sigh as he found it still in place. Taking it off, he undid the straps and felt inside. Money, yes. Two passports, yes. And phone.

In the shadow of the shed the screen created a small pool of light. Gil began tapping...

K. Francisco. Ushuaia. 00.00. J

2

Ushuaia, the following afternoon

A long jetty stretched out south-eastwards from Ushuaia town into the grey waters of the Beagle Channel, in the middle of which was the invisible frontier between Argentina and Chile. Beyond this, to the south, lay the snow-capped peaks of Chile's Isla Navarino and beyond that – seven hundred miles of hazardous ocean beyond – the tip of the frozen continent. Moored at the jetty was the *MS Sturlanga*. A snake of passengers, brightly clad in the dull afternoon, advanced slowly from a clutch of coaches towards the gangway. All but one were gazing up at the five decks that towered above them, their home for the next two weeks. The exception, a grey-bearded man in a blue baseball cap and yellow cagoule, gazed over his shoulder at the opposite quayside before breaking away from the line.

'Joe,' called the woman he'd left, 'where you goin'?'

'Just over there. It's a three-master,' he replied, without turning his head. 'Won't be a minute.'

'Get back 'ere, Joseph. They said walk straight to the boat.' But he was already out of earshot, eyes running keenly over the elegant curves of the old schooner moored in the inner harbour. 'Joseph!'

'Couldn't walk straight if he tried,' muttered someone in the queue, observing the man's limp. A ripple of laughter among her neighbours didn't help placate Joseph's wife, but a young man in a check shirt approached her.

'It's OK, madam. We've seen him. Best wait here till husband come back.' He was one of the ship's crew that had met them on the coaches. This one had an East European accent. Despite the bracing southern air, they were all coatless and all wore check shirts as a kind of informal uniform. Though she did as suggested, she was still visibly agitated.

'He'll be the bloody death of me,' she said, glaring at those nearest in the queue, as though it was their fault.

One of these, a tall gent a few years younger than the arguing couple and, in green wax jacket and yellow corduroys, dressed more for Tunbridge Wells than Tierra del Fuego, turned to the similarly tall man behind him.

'Not a very good advert for England,' he whispered, looking glum. Having heard each other's Home Counties accents on the bus, they'd stood together in the queue and started chatting. Even before boarding, natural herding by nationality had occurred and, in the case of the English at least, by class too. 'Better avoid those two in the bar tonight.'

The other nodded. He was a man of early retirement age wearing a crumpled linen jacket and a battered straw hat complete with a distinctive red feather in the band.

'You're not wrong,' he muttered. 'But I'll be in the cabin catching up with the cricket.'

'Oh yes'. The younger man's face lit up, bright eyes and ready smile beneath a shock of curly dark hair giving him a somewhat saintly appearance. 'The Cape Town test, isn't it? I'd forgotten. Heard any score?'

'England a hundred-odd for two at lunch.' he glanced at his watch. 'Should be around close of play there now. I'll pop up to the bar with the news lateish on if you like. Deck Eight. Probably a middle order collapse as usual.'

'How do you get the scores?'

'Internet. I'll be buying a wi-fi pass as soon as I get on board.'

'Oh, I see. How much...'

But before he could get more gen from his new friend, another check-shirted crew member beckoned him up the gangway like the next sheep for the dip. After the security scan for weapons or (much more likely) alcohol came the medical check. Short and sweet, this consisted of just confirming his good health and handing in a pre-filled form declaring him fit enough to be risked in one of the remotest parts of the Earth. Short but essential: should anyone be taken seriously ill over the next fortnight, the only two options available to the ship's Medical Officer would be to arrange an emergency helicopter – if one happened to be near enough – or advise the Captain to declare the ship an ambulance and divert the other 499 disgruntled passengers to South Georgia – or back to Ushuaia.

Declared both secure and fit, the saintly one found himself guided to a desk where a young Asian woman he judged to be Filipina took his photograph and relieved him of his passport in exchange for a newly printed ID card. This she slid into a bright red lanyard before handing it to him.

'Very handsome photo, Mr Pound,' she said.

Hieronymus Pound examined it with some irritation, accepting that the weary face – not unlike his father's just before death, he thought – must be his own.

'I bet you say that to all the passengers,' he responded, bringing back the beatific smile.

It wasn't so much the image as the name that irked him. While 'Pound' was in small print, above it the name 'HIERONYMUS' appeared in large capital letters. If passengers were expected to address each other by their first names – very twenty-first century, he noted – he'd have opted for the usual 'Harry'.

While some might have been put off by the extra bureaucracy involved in a cruise to Antarctica, Harry had actually been encouraged by it. Less *hoi polloi*, he'd judged, more serious travellers – and no children! Just the title of the holiday, 'An Expedition to the Remote Antarctic Peninsula' should be enough to put off the sun cream and *sangría* brigade. Not that he was averse to either in the right context, which for him would be a hill walk and a shady Spanish bar respectively. No, it was the type of cruise and the type of passengers he was keen to avoid. Truth to tell, if left to his own devices he wouldn't have come on a cruise at all, opting instead for a fortnight by the Med – Greece, Italy, Spain, any would do to get away from the madness that seemed to have engulfed his life.

In normal times, holidays hadn't been a priority; business came first. But for Harry Pound these were not normal times. Even he admitted the Devon affair had taken it out of him. He wasn't his old self. And his business wasn't his old business. In fact, funding apart, it wasn't really *his* business any more. Such was his celebrity status that the property consultancy's clients had become more interested in meeting the hero of the hour than buying or selling their houses. It was Sami, his young assistant, who'd come up with an alternative business plan, one that cashed in on Sami's own skill at encouraging those recently arrived in England to venture out into their adopted country. Well, for those recently arrived with enough money to pay the frankly eye-watering prices for their guided tours. Sami would manage the publicity, bookings and logistics, while Harry did what he was best at: explaining every corner of the English countryside, every dramatic event that had unfolded therein and every bizarre tradition that still occupied the mysterious locals – to those eager to learn. Given Sami's own background, these were mostly Asian families from the Midlands intrigued by the wealthy natives forming their own new customer base.

With 'Pound & Khatri Tours' humming along nicely, Harry had easily acceded to pressure from friends – and from Sami – to take advantage of a gap in their programme and escape for a break. Less easily he'd agreed to a cruise, his first. Good food, distractions, fresh air, they'd said, before ominously adding what they clearly regarded as a bonus: 'And you never know, Harry, you might meet a nice young woman.' Harry's idea of a nice, young woman didn't extend to the sort that regarded crass entertainment and endless buffets as a reasonable basis for a relaxing holiday. In fact, Harry's idea of a relaxing holiday didn't involve women at all – nice or not, young or old. Hence the idea of a manly Antarctic 'expedition', hence a hellish twelve-hour flight to Argentina, a jet-lagged one-night stay in Buenos Aires and another three-hour flight down here to the end of the world. Where, much to Harry's surprise, he found himself in the younger contingent among 500-odd passengers, more or less equally split between the sexes, being sedately processed aboard what was, for the cruising business, a modest-sized vessel.

Placing the cabin card in his top pocket, he glanced around in vain for the cricket fan before trudging off with a shrug in search of his cabin. Deck Four, forward, port side. Waiting there for him was his wheelie-case, also modest in size compared to most. And his bed.

*

A bump stirred him. Then a sway and a crash.

'What the..?' muttered Harry, turning into the wall on one side of the bed before swinging his legs over the other and onto the floor. Which was moving. Oh yes, cabin. Boat. Swaying to the porthole, he stared at an angry grey sky, below which churned waves whose white tops passed unnervingly close by. But we shouldn't be sailing till seven, he thought. His watch was just visible in the semi-darkness. Five past nine? Bugger, what time did they say for dinner?

Ten minutes later, having finally tracked down the restaurant on Deck Five aft, he stood at its entrance struggling to process the information coming from the polite but firm steward.

'Yes, some late people are still dining, sir, but last entry was at nine o' clock. Perhaps you like to join most of the passengers in the Panorama Lounge for Captain's address?' Harry stared blankly. Unavoidably for someone fascinated by language, half of his mind had started to wonder which part of Eastern Europe would use the phrase 'late people', while the other half focused on the disappointment felt in his stomach. 'Deck Eight, forward, sir.'

The panorama that gave the double-height lounge its name remained invisible to Harry as he strained to see beyond the heads of the other passengers pressed at the back of the throng. He could hear though. Currently speaking was a woman with a slight Scandinavian intonation and associated lilt, but in perfect English.

'Drake Passage, named after the famous English explorer and pirate has, like him, two types of character: Drake Lake and Drake Shake. As you will have already noticed, the forecast for our crossing is Drake Shake.' Laughter duly passed around the lounge. 'So as you move around the ship please hold onto the hand rails and accept the help of the crew. We expect to reach calmer waters the day after tomorrow.'

With that she began speaking in French, which – as far as Harry could tell – was just as fluent as her English. The man next to him – black, stocky and so short his view of proceedings must have been negligible – glanced at his watch and then at Harry.

'Best make the bar before the rush, eh?' It was an American accent.

'Oh, have I missed the Captain?' asked Harry.

'That *was* the Captain. Want me to fill you in over a beer?'

*

'Lennox,' said the American, offering his hand as they sat with full glasses on the starboard side to see the last of the sun. There was more hair on the back of his big hands than on his head. Strong too, as Harry noted from his grip. Below a neat grey moustache sparkled a full set of pure white teeth. 'But then you can see that from this.' He indicated the pass dangling from his neck. With some dismay Harry had already noticed that virtually everyone was wearing them. His own still sat safely in his pocket.

'Oh yes,' he said. 'Harry.'

'I'm from Boston.'

Harry nodded but said nothing. Not having eaten since a snack on the plane, he was scanning around in search of snacks.

'Massachusetts,' added Lennox.

'Ah, yes. I'd guessed it wasn't Boston, Lincolnshire.'

Lennox laughed loudly and sharply.

'British sense of humour, right?'

'I'm from near Oxford. Um, Oxfordshire.'

Lennox repeated the laugh, harsh like a fox's bark, drawing a few stares. Passengers were now streaming out of the Panorama Lounge.

'I made my money in maritime, down on Cape Cod. Lotta money to be made down there. What about you, Harry?'

Having met a fair few Americans in his time, Harry wasn't as taken aback as many would be at Lennox's directness. Nor his assumptions: after all, it wasn't everyone who could afford the luxury of an Antarctic cruise.

'I'm in property,' he said, forgetting for a moment he no longer was. 'What you'd call real estate.'

'An' I hear real estate values are pretty high over there. Say, you look a bit pale, Harry. Not a good sailor?'

'It's not that. I missed dinner. Fast asleep. Do you know if they do snacks in here?'

'Just potato chips at the bar. And there's a line there now. Hey, you know what? Maisie and I got a coupla subs in the cabin. I'll get you one, Harry. Ham and cheese, seems kinda standard for Argentina.'

'No, no, I'll be...'

But he'd already set off. In the few minutes he was away, Harry indulged in one of his favourite pastimes: simply observing others. Listening to the mix of languages and accents came as a welcome relief from the wall-to-wall English around his home in the Cotswolds. After the hassle of the getting here, a sense of holiday at last came over him. There were Americans, British, Germans, a small knot of French, a few East Europeans. No Spanish to be heard, which he found strange here on the edge of Latin America. Shame: he'd hoped to practise his own Spanish, rusty after years back in England. Maybe they had their own cruise ships. One or two people in search of a table looked over at the dapper gent in the pastel-green shirt and chinos, hastily retrieved from his cabin by Harry between failed restaurant visit and failed lounge visit, but the second beer told them the other seat was occupied. A useful trick, thought Harry, perfectly happy to drink alone. Worth buying an extra pint. And, oddly enough, pints they seemed to be.

Two tables away, one or two French speakers unravelled themselves from the knot to reveal a pile of expensive-looking equipment – video cameras, microphones and the like – surrounding the alpha male: tall, even while seated, square-jawed, blue-eyed, curly-haired and the centre of attention, especially female attention. Sharp words were being exchanged between him and one of the others, but before Harry could focus on them Lennox returned with an unopened roll, which Harry gratefully set about while the American summarised the Captain's address.

'Like most folks I was lookin' round for the skipper when she was there all the time. Captain Thommessen, first female captain of the line and damn proud of it too. Did you catch a glimpse?' Mouth full, Harry nodded. 'Put it this way – you wouldn't mess with her. She introduced the maritime crew – all guys, all Norwegian like her, far as I could make out. Then the expedition leader took over. Did you know we were on an expedition?'

'Mm.'

'News to me. Anyhow, he's a soft-spoken German – first I ever came across, wouldn't trust the guy an inch – name of Stefan, can't be more 'n thirty. Some o' the ladies started swoonin' when he jumped up. Then the whole expedition team took a bow. That's the kids in the check shirts. Turns out they're all scientists o' some sort. Geologists, *bio*logists, *hydro*logists, *climato*logists, you name the ology, they're right here on this ship. There was even a political scientist. Now ain't that a contradiction in terms? Hey, I didn't ask, Harry – maybe you studied some of these things. Oxford, you said. Oxford University?'

Harry hesitated. Back home it'd sound like boasting but, well, he'd already let one untruth slip out.

'Yes, I did go to Oxford actually.'

'I knew it. That accent. I skipped college from sixteen myself. What d'you study, Harry?'

He hesitated a little longer this time.

'Political science.'

'Ha!' Rather than stares, Lennox's fox laugh drew grins now. People had been drinking.

'Thanks for the roll, Lennox,' said Harry. 'Can I buy you another beer?'

Waiting at the bar, Harry wondered why on earth he'd lied again. Well, not a complete lie. He'd read PPE – Politics, Philosophy and Economics – none of which he really regarded as science. He recalled a comment from one friend who'd been on a few cruises: on board no one knows you from Adam, so you can become anyone you want – and many often do. He'd have to be watchful, of himself as much as others. Thinking of England suddenly reminded him of the cricket and the man in the queue. Lateish in the bar, he'd said. Walking back with the drinks he looked around but couldn't spot him.

'Is there only one bar?' he asked Lennox as he resumed his seat.

'Yeah. Well, I saw a little one on Deck Nine, but this is the main drinkin' hole. Why?'

'Just looking for someone, another Englishman.'

'Not the loud guy with the louder wife?'

'No, this chap was on his own. What loud guy?'

'Oh, you were asleep, weren't you? Well, you missed quite a scene earlier on. Right here. This English couple were really goin' at it. Seems he wanders off ignoring her all the time. Hell, one look at her and you could see why.' Harry realised this must have been the man who left the queue on the quayside. 'I reckon he'd been at the bottle before they got on board. Her too maybe. Throws her drink at him, broken glass all over the floor. He walks out onto the deck. Staggers more like. She follows him. One of the bartenders follows 'em both. We all look at each other. Maisie says it's like a TV soap, only with English accents. Say, do you Brits have soaps?'

'I believe so,' said Harry. He heard the sneer in his own voice. No more to drink tonight, he told himself, and changed the subject.

Soon he'd made his excuses and left Lennox having 'just one more' while he swayed his own way up to Deck Nine, feeling a little queasy now. His cabin and a sea-sickness pill were calling, but he felt some obligation to try and find the cricket man.

*

The Polar Bar, barely justified the name: just a counter, a shelf of bottles and a coffee machine. With no sign of his man and the two bar stools occupied, Harry was about to call it a day when he caught the tempting whiff of good coffee and ordered one. Wary of the beverage swaying in his hand, he remembered the advice to plant yourself amidships in rough weather and ventured out on deck where a comfy sofa fitted the bill. The on-deck thermometer read two degrees. With the breeze of the Southern Ocean on his cheeks, a rug around his legs, an unopened book on his lap and the warm cup in his hand, he was just beginning to let his mind wander to the voyage ahead when angry voices drifted through the doors behind him, shortly followed by angry steps to his right. As soon as the yellow coat and big grey beard swayed into view he realised the couple on the bar stools had been the argumentative northerners Lennox had reminded him about. Clearly the row had still not subsided and, keen not to get involved, Harry made a point of looking the other way. To his surprise though, the man, who was alone now, passed a polite comment on Harry's book and wished him goodnight before disappearing into the gathering gloom.

Not long afterwards Harry headed off to his cabin, unaware how significant the last ten minutes would prove to be – to himself, to other passengers and to several others thousands of miles away.

3

Harry had vague memories of a soporific German voice (male) a search for the off switch (unsuccessful) and an adjustment of the volume control (successful). All the rest was darkness, motion, distant rattles and sleep. A lot of sleep. When he eventually squinted at his watch, on this occasion it read six-fifteen. Morning? Evening? A tap on his smartphone gave the answer: 18:15. Could he really have been under that duvet for nearly twenty hours? Just to be sure, he read the date too: yes, at least it was only the next day.

'Well, Louise,' he muttered to himself. 'You were right.' The tablets for motion sickness worked by knocking you out, she'd said. They were the real deal. He must thank her: an excuse for an e-mail. Sitting in the dark on the edge of the bed, riffling his hair into life, Harry's thoughts jumped effortlessly back thirty years to another small bed in another small room. Louise – his tutor, his confidente and suddenly, unexpectedly, his lover – had awoken with his movements and they'd shared that startled, silent look, both slightly alarmed at what they'd done. They'd both known she was the one out of order but the guilt felt equally shared. Unspoken and unagreed, they'd simply avoided each other for a week.

When normal service resumed it was as though it had never happened. Debates, challenges, the regular cut and thrust of tutorials – it all carried on with the same combination of objectivity and intensity as before. No intimate glances in seminars, no secret notes in the margins. Harry at least was sure none of his fellow students suspected anything. He certainly hadn't told anyone. After finals – and after Louise had met the man she'd eventually marry – that should have been the end of it: leave Oxford, move on.

But somehow it wasn't.

Whenever world events demanded an opinion, they'd be back in touch to share reactions, float ideas, offer comments. Dolly the sheep, Princess Diana, the euro, the Balkans, 9/11... Louise would be the calm analyst to Harry's knee-jerk reactionary. With time he'd usually come round to her side, learn to pull back, see the big picture. Recently, though, the moralistic knives had come out. Louise would point out the discrepancy between Harry's purported concern for the built-in unfairness of the property market and his relentless success in exploiting it. Harry would remind Louise that her attachment to religious festivals, especially those involving extravagant family gatherings, sat rather awkwardly with her complete lack of faith in any kind of god.

In fact, he realised as he squeezed his ample frame into the cabin's compact shower, it had been well before Christmas when he'd let Louise know about the cruise and she'd recommended the sea-sick pills – followed up by a reminder to be polite to strangers. (Why did his friends keep mentioning this?) She'd be well out of festive mode by now. As the low-pressure, lukewarm water gently washed away sleep, he began to compose an e-mail in his head. The morality of cruising in Antarctica. Where did he stand? All this water he was using, for example: well, there's hardly much demand down here, is there? Were the cruise ships polluting the place? As he towelled himself down, he determined to raid the ship's library for some insight with which to dazzle his friendly adversary. He was already looking forward to the usual to and fro on a subject she'd surely have an outspoken opinion on.

*

Refreshed by sleep and relieved by the steady floor and calmer seascape, he was soon also looking forward to a normal evening. The cabin's TV was devoted principally to the cruise itself and, after checking on the bow camera for the state of the sea ahead (a little calmer) and whether land was yet in sight (it wasn't), he found the day's schedule. Not good news. Tonight's dinner would be 'formal'. While no dinner jacket was required, he recalled from the welter of pre-departure information that there'd be allocated seating – so he'd be stuck with people that someone somewhere had decided he might get on with. A nightmare. Was there a separate self-service restaurant for the socially reluctant? Apparently not. Harry's empty stomach told him he'd got to face the music.

So, after an emergency chocolate bar and a slightly less frantic scramble than the previous evening, Harry trudged up to Deck Five and took his place at the table for four to which the steward directed him. He was the last to arrive.

A man, probably in his sixties and sporting large spectacles beneath an extravagant comb-over, sat opposite a woman perhaps twenty years younger. Wife? Daughter? Probably the former, thought Harry. She was sturdily built but with dainty, dyed-blonde curls, carefully dressed and in possession of a pair of clear blue eyes that gave her the benevolent look of a social worker sympathising with distraught parents. Next to her sat a woman of similar age but with sharply contrasting looks: pale, gaunt and half-hidden behind long, dark hair that had had no recent encounter with a brush. God, he thought, is she a single I've been matched with? As he sat opposite, introducing himself and apologising for his lateness, the pale lady defiantly continued to peruse the menu, while the others greeted him.

'Pleased to meet you', said Comb-Over, 'I'm Vernon.' Harry

immediately knew he was seated next to a Londoner, but whether nearer the stockbroker or barrow-boy end of the social scale he wasn't yet sure. Don't judge, he reminded himself.

Blue Eyes offered a limp hand across the table.

'Fiona,' she said. With no word forthcoming from her neighbour, Fiona continued. 'And this is Danielle. We're not a pair of those lesbians. Have you seen the two French girls swanning around holding hands? Disgusting is what I call it.'

With so much information to process – not least that he'd guessed the pairing wrongly – Harry hesitated long enough for Danielle to raise her head and utter a reluctant 'Hi' before resuming her menu study.

'No, I can't say I have,' he replied. 'Are you both from Ireland?' That this was Fiona's background was as clear as Waterford crystal. But before either could answer, the wine waiter, who'd already served the other three, asked Harry what he'd care to drink.

'Do you have a Rioja?' he asked.

'I'm afraid we don't, sir, but I can recommend the Malbec. By the bottle is a good deal – we keep it till your next meal if requested.'

'Bottle of Malbec it is then.'

'Of course it is,' said Vernon as the waiter left. 'They load Malbec by the barrel in Buenos Aires. Over fifty thousand acres of the stuff in Argentina. Mendoza's the wine centre, out west, near the border with Chile.'

This little speech, especially the 'fifty thaasand' helped Harry slot Vernon squarely in the barrow-boy set of Londoners.

'You know a lot about wine, Vernon,' commented Fiona without approval.

'I know a lot about South America too,' said Vernon, oblivious to her tone. 'Used to be a geography teacher.' So much for his guess at this chap's social standing, admitted Harry to himself. 'Been swottin' up on Antarctica. Do you know which island we'll see first?'

Before the human atlas could enlighten the group on this point, much to Harry's relief Danielle finally spoke up to wind the conversation back.

'No, Harry, I'm originally from Scotland, but like Fiona I live near London now.'

'Both of us lost our dear husbands,' expanded Fiona without invitation, 'my Bernard at the peak of his powers as a GP. And now we're both members of the local club for lost souls – or book club, as it's officially known. Dani here kindly invited me along on this adventure.'

'What about you, Harry?' asked Danielle, after a pause.

Well educated, Harry noted. After letting a couple of half-truths escape his lips yesterday, he'd resolved to play it straight.

'I live in the Cotswolds, but you may notice a hint of Liverpool. I was born there.'

This mutual interrogation was interrupted by the arrival of Harry's wine and the placing of food orders. This done, Fiona, who'd been shuffling in her seat since she last spoke, fixed Harry with such an intense stare from those blue eyes that he found himself leaning away.

'So, Harry, you're on holiday on your own. Are you another one like Vernon here who's given his wife a blessed break while he plays at being an explorer?'

'No wife back home,' he said simply, hoping that would close the matter. His hopes were dashed.

'Girlfriend then?'

He shrugged in a non-committal sort of way.

'So you're all alone. Why's that then?' continued Fiona. Harry got the impression she'd run through these same questions in a hundred previous interrogations of solitary males.

'Do I need a reason to be in the state we're all born in and most of us die in?'

With this, Danielle's static features creased into an ill-disguised smirk.

'Ha!' she said. '*Touché!* He's got you there, Fi. Leave the young man alone, now. Not everyone bows to your wisdom on matters matrimonial.'

The arrival of food put a line under these opening skirmishes. With two more formal meals scheduled among the same dinner companions, Harry realised it was going to be competitive and was pleased to have scored an early point against the plain-speaking Irish woman, albeit with the assistance of her enigmatic friend. Setting about his mushroom orzo with appreciation and enthusiasm, he wondered why these two contrasting characters had ended up on a cruise together. The conversation, however, had taken a course of more immediate interest.

'Do you think that poor man from Cabin 642's fallen overboard?' asked Fiona.

'It's the obvious conclusion,' suggested Vernon, 'unless he's hiding on purpose – but then what chance has anyone got to hide for two weeks on a ship he can't escape from?'

'Wait a minute,' said Harry, when he'd swallowed the latest mouthful. 'What man? What cabin?'

'All those announcements all day,' said Vernon. 'You must have heard them: Would Mr Challinor from Cabin 642 please report to Reception at once?'

'I'm afraid I've been out of it. Seasick pills, exhaustion, fast asleep.'

'Surely you heard them in your cabin. Can't turn the darned speaker off.'

'But you can turn the volume way down.'

Before Vernon, visibly irritated at someone knowing a trick he didn't, could come back with some extra fact, Fiona had taken charge.

'Oh something dreadful's happened I'm sure, Harry,' she said with relish. 'It started just after breakfast. Would the occupant of Cabin 642 please report to Reception? Then would Mr Challinor from Cabin 642 please report to any member of the crew at once? Then would Mr Joseph Challinor make himself known to anyone at all?' Harry's mind immediately turned to the absent cricket fan in the straw hat, only to be turned back again by Fiona's next version of the tannoy announcements. The woman seemed to have an astounding memory. 'And finally would Mr Joseph Challinor please report to the medical centre on Deck Four where his wife is waiting.' He was pretty sure Straw Hat was on his own.

'Too late to turn the old girl round,' said Vernon. 'The ship. Too late to initiate standard emergency procedure for man overboard – pinpoint location where he went in, turn her round and return to same spot. If he went over before breakfast it's too late, far too late. He's a gonner, I'd say.'

The rest of the meal followed in a somewhat depressed atmosphere as the horror of being alone at sea – and especially alone amid the cold, mountainous seas of Drake Passage – disturbed their thoughts. Dessert was over and coffees ordered when a ripple of loud chatter was heard to spread from one end of the restaurant. Members of the crew seemed to be distributing something to each table. Eventually it arrived at theirs. It was an A4 sheet bearing a head-and-shoulders photograph of a man, below which the word 'MISSING' preceded the following stark request from the Captain:

Mr Joseph Challinor, British, 54 (above) was reported missing at 08:11 this morning 23rd February. I am very concerned for his safety. If anyone has seen Mr Challinor since 22:15 on 22nd February or has any relevant

information, please report to me or to any member of the crew at once.
Capt U Thommessen

The same message appeared in French, German and Spanish. Vernon had read out the English. Even before he'd finished, Harry pushed back his chair and stood up.

'Excuse me,' he said. 'I must see the Captain.'

*

Dabbing her lips with a napkin, Fiona took charge.

'I'll follow him,' she said, rising. 'You two wait in the bar.'

Five minutes later they'd regrouped. As soon as Fiona had seen the woman from Reception deliver Harry to a small meeting room tucked away in a corner of the bar behind the piano, she beckoned the others to a table nearby and sat down.

'Danielle,' she ordered, 'get our drinks, including a glass of that Welbeck for Harry...'

'Malbec.'

'... so we can catch him when he comes out.'

Drinks assembled, they discussed the situation. Or rather Fiona and Vernon did.

'Maybe Harry saw the man go over,' suggested Fiona.

'Don't be ridiculous,' said Vernon. 'He'd have alerted someone, wouldn't he? It's more likely he overheard his wife threatening him. I didn't like the look of her. There was a case in Walthamstow in the nineties when a small woman...'

'Never mind all that. What's important is we get the inside track on this one. I can see you and I are the same, Vernon. We're both know-alls,' Vernon choked a little on his beer; Danielle sipped her Pinot Grigio. 'You know everything about the outside world, I know about the inside world.' She tapped her head. 'The case of Joseph Challinor will be the talk of all the boat tomorrow and we need to be on top of it. With Harry's help, we may even crack the case.'

'I think the Security Officer will take that on. While the Captain has overall responsibility for everyone on board, he – sorry she – delegates...'

'Danielle, are you keeping an eye on the office door from there?'

'I can see it,' said Danielle and took another sip.

Fiona's glass remained untouched.

*

The meeting room comprised just a desk occupied by a computer screen, and three chairs. As Harry was led in, his first impression was how incongruous such a mundane reminder of the everyday world looked against a view through the window of the endlessly rolling Southern Ocean. His second was that there was barely room for the two occupants, let alone himself. The nearer of the two he recognised as Captain Thommessen, altogether larger than she'd appeared in the Panorama Lounge. Blonde locks held tightly back in a pony tail, one high cheek bone adorned with an old scar, muscular frame held under control by an immaculate uniform, she reminded Harry of an Olympic athlete about to receive an award.

'Mr Pound,' she said, 'thank you for coming forward. I'm Captain Thommessen and this is Nils, my Security Officer.' Harry was impressed: formal, brief, personal responsibility to the fore. Nils rose as far as the seat would allow to offer his hand. Younger than his boss, but not in such good shape and with a drooping mouth that seemed to match drooping shoulders, he struggled to raise even a polite smile. 'Please have a seat if you can fit in. Now, was this the man you saw last night sometime?'

Nils had turned the screen to face Harry.

'Yes, that's him.'

'How can you be sure?' asked Nils.

'I was standing near him and his wife when we were boarding and saw them together again in the Polar Bar last night. At least I assume it's his wife.'

Nils clicked the mouse and another face appeared.

'This woman?'

'Yes.'

'His wife.'

'How is she?'

'Naturally disturbed,' said Nils.

'My medical staff are looking after her,' added the Captain.

'Now, please tell me what you saw last night and at what time,' continued Nils.

Harry ran through the short encounter.

'I'd say I went out on deck about ten fifteen,' he added.

Nils examined a list on screen.

'Your cabin card was scanned for your coffee at eleven minutes past,' he said. 'Can you remember what the Challinors were drinking?'

Harry refrained from suggesting the same list would probably show that.

'Yes. He had a coffee. I didn't notice hers.'

'That's correct. His wife's was a wine.'

He felt he'd passed some sort of test.

Nils went on: 'And how would you describe Mr Challinor's, er, condition when he came on deck?'

'I'd describe it as calm and coherent. Which surprised me, as I'd assumed from their arguing they were both drunk.'

The Captain and Security Officer exchanged a quick glance.

'You're sure of that?' asked the Captain.

'I'm sure that was my impression. I noticed he was pretty steady on his feet too, given the ship was still pitching and I still felt a bit queasy.'

'Ill,' Captain Thommessen said to Nils, who nodded before

making a few more clicks and showing Harry a still image from a CCTV camera.

'Is this you?' he said, pointing at the only figure in the shot, sitting in semi-darkness beneath a blanket with the light from the bar window behind him. The time on the image was 22:20.

Harry leaned forward.

'Looks like it. That's where I was sitting and the time is right.'

'Our security cameras operate on a sweep basis and this is one of only two images we have of you there. This must have been after Mr Challinor left you. Here's the other a few minutes later. As you can see, someone has just passed you on their way back into the corridor on the other side from the bar. Unfortunately not a very clear image of them. Now, this is important. Did you see Mr Challinor return inside?'

Harry hesitated. He understood why it was important.

'No,' he said after a moment. 'It's true – one or two people did pass me on the other side, but I didn't pay much attention. I've no reason to think any of them was Mr Challinor.'

'Why not?'

'Well, I suppose I'd have noticed the bright yellow coat and the beard and he's quite tall anyway, isn't he?'

Nils glanced once again at his boss.

'You say one or two, Mr Pound,' she said. 'Which was it?'

He shook his head. 'I'm not sure. Sorry.'

'And you say you think Mr Challinor didn't return. Do you think or do you know?'

He pursed his lips. Harry Pound was well aware how such investigations hang on a witness's words. To his own cost.

'All I can say is I wasn't aware I saw Mr Challinor again. In fact I'm pretty sure I didn't see him again.'

She raised her eyebrows wordlessly.

'Ninety per cent sure,' he said.

She pushed back in her chair.

'Very good,' she said, without consulting Nils. 'That's all. You've been most helpful. Nils may have to ask you to sign a statement confirming what you've just told us, if that's all right.' He nodded. 'Is there anything you'd like to ask us?'

Harry stroked his chin.

'There is actually. Are the Challinors from Lancashire?'

It was Nils's turn to raise his eyebrows. 'Just a moment,' he said, clicking through a few more files. 'Why do you ask?'

'Accents are something of a hobby of mine,' he said.

'Here it is,' said Nils, carefully turning the screen away from Harry. 'Yes, you're right. They're from...'

'Blackburn?'

'Chorley.'

'A few miles away.'

'How did you know that?' asked Captain Thommessen.

'Lots of rolling Rs and book to rhyme with spook, not luck.'

'Very impressive,' said Captain Thommessen, with a hint of suspicion in her voice. 'But of course you know where I'm from.'

'I don't know what part of Norway, of course, but I'd guess you learnt your English either in America or in the south-west of England.'

This seemed to surprise and please her in equal measure.

'Spot on, Mr Pound. I studied maritime law at Bristol and then went to the US. What gives me away?'

'More rolling Rs, Captain, but nothing else northern at all.'

'Hm. What about Nils here?'

Harry looked at the Security Officer with his head on one side.

'I'd guess you learnt most of your excellent English in Norway,' he concluded.

A wry smile spread over Nils's tight features.

'Correct,' he said.

The Captain thanked Harry again and shook his hand as he squeezed out of the little office. Before she closed the door, he heard her explaining to her officer the difference between 'disturbed' and 'distraught'.

Pretending not to notice his recent dinner companions beyond the piano, Harry walked swiftly to the starboard side and down to his cabin. He needed quiet to try and bring to the front of his mind the one thing about those few minutes on deck he felt was significant but which lurked irritatingly at the back. It wasn't to come till later.

4

The following morning, Yorkshire

Some 250 years before the *MS Sturlanga* rounded Cape Horn to head south, a much smaller and alarmingly more fragile vessel had battled under wind power alone past the same point, but on a westerly heading. It had been many months since *HMS Endeavour* had set sail from Plymouth and many more since its captain, James Cook, had last set foot in Great Ayton, his boyhood home tucked beneath the northern slopes of the Cleveland Hills. In this same Yorkshire village on the morning after Hieronymus Pound had sat pondering the events of his first two days as a cruise passenger, there was another connection with the Southern Ocean.

Money was to be made in Great Ayton from its link to Captain Cook, and a young man slipping as quietly as possible into his modest car outside the Endeavour Café intended to make his fair share. Josh Burnet had never meant to run a café. He'd never even meant to bake cakes, let alone Captain Cook Carrot Cake or the even more popular Seafaring Sponge Cake. He hadn't dreamt he'd turn his hand to art either, filling a corner of the eatery with small wooden carvings that bore a passing resemblance – in a modern-arty sort of way – to wind-blown skippers and graceful sailing ships. To be honest, he thought to himself as he turned on the headlights, he couldn't quite remember what he *had* meant to do with his life when he'd been Captain Cook's age growing up in village. Wasn't it rally driver?

The reason he'd crept out so quietly was that it was still an hour before dawn and Paula, his live-in girlfriend and business partner, was still asleep – as many of the neighbours must have been. Got to keep them onside. Instead of a rally driver he'd become the local Casanova, then world traveller, then world saviour (short-lived, that one, and possibly only in his mind) and then... well, is drifter an activity? This unbidden reflection on his previous incarnations was prompted by the ritual of that particular pre-dawn winter's morning. The same date only three years before had slammed into his life's trajectory like a meteorite. Some people – perhaps most – react to tragedy by shutting down, switching off. Josh, his battery already almost expired, had reacted by switching on, by diverting himself with creativity. The house is suddenly empty? So fill it up. No goals in life? So make one. Make lots.

Within ten minutes, he'd pulled up at a lay-by. It still felt like the middle of the night and, as he stepped out to get the items from the boot, significantly colder than down in the village. In the dark cocoon of the car it was easy to forget he'd driven uphill onto the moors. Bag slung over left shoulder and torch in right hand, he set off up the gravel path and through the forest. Soon the gravel turned to flagstones as the trees gave way to a low scrub, beyond which the dull purple of a chilly dawn slowly spread up into a murky sky still unsure about accepting it. Not bad, thought Josh. The three of them had often been up here in worse conditions than this. His favourites were snowy days when it felt like the moors lay on the other side of the world from the village.

Cook's monument itself stands sixty feet tall, its rough stones a shimmering pink that morning as Josh dropped his bag against the railings on the east side to face the dawn. The face of his watch was just visible: a few minutes to sunrise. Time to take the flowers out and, removed from their plastic wrapper, lean them carefully on the southern flank. Next came the beautifully crafted little velvet and leather purse he'd inherited, out of which he lifted a schoolboy compass, equally exquisite in its own way. This he held face up, turning it slightly until the silver needle settled against the letter S. Turning to face the same direction and straightening his back, Josh Burnet caught the glint of the rising sun to his left and began to recite in a soft, low voice:

Art in life.
Art in death.
Art is always with us.
In our hearts.
In our breath.
In all that you bequeath us.

By the last line his voice had begun to crack. Funny, he thought, with no one else there. Just him this year.

Actually, that wasn't quite true.

5

Same morning, MS Sturlanga

Apart from the small Polar Bar, an equally compact gym and the lift, Deck Nine was open to the elements, including its jacuzzi and helipad either side of the funnel. That morning those elements had turned more favourable, the thermometer showed just above zero and the deck was awash with passengers making a valiant attempt to walk off their ample breakfasts. The westerly winds that had shaken up Drake Passage for forty-eight hours had veered to a northerly, making the port side the breeziest. Nevertheless this is where most loitered in hope of spotting land. Almost all wore the bright green waterproof coats issued as part of the cost of the cruise. Among them were Harry, Lennox and Maisie. Like Harry, Lennox's wife had been largely cabin-bound during the Drake Shake.

'Oh, that's a whole lot better, Lennie,' she said. 'Food inside me and wind in my hair.' Also African-American, her slim build, smooth complexion and jet-black hair made her look at least ten years younger than her husband. 'How 'bout you, Harry?'

'Certainly glad to be out,' he replied. In fact he'd been up and about for a while, making good use of the twenty-four-hour wi-fi pass he'd bought. During an early stroll on deck he'd spotted Vernon by one rail and Danielle, minus Fiona, by the other, but had scuttled past unseen. 'I wonder how soon we'll see land.'

'Can't be long,' said Lennox. 'That German guy on the speakers said we'd been making good headway and maybe, just maybe, there'll be a landing later on today.'

'About time,' said Maisie. 'I want to see if they take US dollars out here – that's all I got.'

'Honey, I told you, there ain't no 'they' in Antarctica, unless you're planning to buy a beak off a penguin. There ain't no shops.'

'Well, what we here for then?'

'We've been through this a hundred times, sweetheart. Your purse is in the cabin safe and that's where it's staying. Harry, I've done my best – can you explain it to her?'

Whether Harry could have got Maisie to appreciate the vast, wonderful emptiness of the southern continent was to remain an unknown, since a shout from someone a further forward along the rail drew everyone's attention.

'Land!'

'No, it's a boat.'

'No, wait, it's an iceberg.'

Cue a hundred cameras.

'An iceberg? May the Lord protect us. I wonder if the Captain's seen it?'

The Irish accent announced the arrival on deck of Fiona, now behind Harry's right shoulder.

'Oh, morning. Don't worry,' said Harry as he turned round. 'As we're just off Antarctica, I'd imagine Captain Thommessen might be ready for icebergs.'

'They'd be on the radar anyway,' pointed out Vernon, following behind Fiona. 'At least.'

'Captain Thommessen is it, Harry?' asked Fiona. 'Is she your friend now?'

Harry introduced the Lennoxes to Fiona and Vernon. 'No Danielle this morning?' he asked.

'She's reserving our seats in the lounge. Now, who'd like a coffee and a chat?'

Oddly, the prospect of an intrusive interrogation by Fiona was somehow trumped by taking in one of the strangest sights in the world as, one after another, huge chunks of ice shaped by nature into ever-more fantastic shapes slid silently by. Here was one that looks like a swan, followed by a sports car – specifically, as Vernon observed, a Porsche 911 – and then a grand house, possibly the right size too. With nothing else in view for reference, and distance from the vessel difficult to judge, they couldn't really tell. Eventually Fiona found an ally in Maisie, to whom the chilly air seemed to come as a surprise, and Lennox was duly beckoned inside. As the ice show disappeared beyond the stern, the others eventually followed.

*

The midships section of Deck Five was given over to a zone of low tables and easy chairs, a self-service coffee machine on one side and on the other a children's play area which for 'expedition' cruises served as a map zone. The lounge was already filling up but Fiona had received a message from Danielle telling her where she'd reserved seats.

'How did you do that?' asked Harry, as he sat down. 'I thought there was no mobile signal south of Ushuaia.'

'That there's not,' said Fiona. 'But there's an app you can use on the ship's wi-fi that lets you send a text to another phone number. A lot simpler than e-mail. You see, you don't know everything after all, do you, Harry? It's called What's App... but I don't know why.'

'It just means hello,' said Maisie. 'Kids say it.'

'Say what?'

'Wossup?'

'What?'

'Wossup? Wossap? Same thing.'

Fiona shook her curls.

'Whatever,' she said, as Danielle went off for the coffees. 'Now, Harry, to business. What's the inside story on the case of the missing man?'

Harry looked bemused. He was good at bemused. In this company bemused would become his speciality.

'There's no inside story,' he said, with what he vainly hoped was finality.

'Come on,' persisted Fiona. 'A missing person poster arrived, you left dinner mid-coffee and went into a private room with the Captain.'

Now Lennox and Maisie were interested as well as both Vernon, who knew all this, and a young man at the next table, who didn't.

'It was nothing really. I'd seen the missing man around the time they were interested in, I felt obliged to report it. That's all.' His voice was low. All strained forward to listen. The coffees had arrived but remained untouched.

'Where? When? Were you the last person to see him alive?'

'Well, I don't know that. In fact I don't know he's dead. It was up on Deck Nine, where we've just been.'

'So he wandered past you blind drunk, leaned over the rail to throw up and fell in?'

'I don't know any of that.'

As he too had stooped forward to avoid raising his voice, Harry's cabin card fell out of his top pocket onto the table with a clatter. Before he'd picked it up, Vernon caught sight of the name, leaned back and looked at the ceiling before speaking to no one in particular.

'Yes,' he said, 'That's where I've read that name. Hieronymus Pound.' Harry feared the worst. It came. 'You were in the news a while back. An incident in Devon. A policeman was murdered. You were the hero of the hour, weren't you?'

The others' eyes were all on Harry. Fiona's had all but popped out, but Lennox got in before her.

'Devon, England?' he verified, somewhat unnecessarily.

'What was that name again?' asked Fiona. 'Were you hiding it?'

'Are you really a hero?' asked Maisie.

Harry's eyes were closed as he shook his head, before taking a steady sip from his coffee – a trick he'd learnt when a considered response was called for.

'Ugh, that's disgusting,' he said.

Danielle apologised. 'It's from the free coffee machine.'

'No, I mean thank you for getting it. Now I know.'

'Never mind the coffee. The hero thing!' demanded Fiona.

'Well,' began Harry. 'Yes, that was me in Devon. Yes, England. No, I'm not a hero. Two people died that day and I couldn't save either of them. I'm not proud of it. If anyone acted heroically, it was my assistant, my friend. And yes, I have an odd name, difficult for people to remember, so I just use Harry. It's not a big deal.'

'I remember now,' said Vernon. 'The police said you solved the crime – or an old crime – and if it wasn't for you others would have died too.'

Harry shrugged. 'Actually,' he said.' I've got to catch up on some things while I've got the wi-fi, so if you'll excuse me. Thanks for the coffee.'

The rest of the table fell silent as they considered this new information. Even Fiona. At the next table the young man sat back thoughtfully before tapping on his phone.

*

Back in his cabin, Harry sat at the small desk and immediately wished he's brought a laptop. This phone might be smart but it was clearly designed by youngsters with small fingers. Even if it condescended to recognise his own indelicate digits as belonging to a human, it rarely knew what he was trying to type. Or pretended it didn't. Nevertheless his earlier attempts had at least revealed the expected collapse in England's middle order and the Cape Town test was hurtling towards another defeat. His mention of his assistant Sami had reminded him that he ought to check in on business – as well as giving him an excuse to escape the attentions of his fellow passengers. An e-mail from the very man lay in his inbox. After a couple of mis-clicks he managed to open it and the reassuring formality of his young colleague immediately cheered him up.

Dear Mr Pound

I hope your cruise is progressing nicely. I have borrowed from the library a map of Antarctica and am ready to point the pin at your location if you would be so kind as to inform me.

Update! Everything is in order here and also Bristol fashion:

> 1-Day Tour N02 'The Stately Homes of Nottinghamshire: Wealth and Woodland' has been booked for the 15th as agreed. My local contact has asked if a wider choice of jams could be made available for the scones.

> Our advertising for 3-Day Tour M05 on Anglo-Saxon England still requires a name. May I humbly suggest 'Midland England: the Very Edge of Darkness'? Our clientele enjoys a mild threat. And even more humbly I wonder why you plan to begin at a bicycle shop in Brownhills?

> I hope you approve of my new Tour Coding System, which cleverly suggests we have more tours than we truly do.

> A letter has arrived for you from Messrs Hook and Tysoe (Solicitors) marked 'Private & Confidential', which of course I have left on your desk unopened.

That is all for now. Cecilia has asked me to inquire if you have yet met any unattached ladies on board the vessel. I myself would not ask such a question.

Yours sincerely,

S Khatri

Hook and Tysoe rang a bell, but from eight thousand miles away a very faint one. Taking a deep breath, Harry began tapping in his reply. After a ten-minute battle with both the virtual keyboard and its virtually incomprehensible attempts to correct him, he had before him a paragraph that at least was grammatically correct:

Dear Sami. Thank you for your efficient update. I agree with all your suggestions. The bike shop is named after an Anglo-Saxon kingdom. Please open the confidential letter. Is it possible to send me a photograph? Please tell your girlfriend there are far too many unattached females aboard. My location is near Deception Island. PS The verb is to pinpoint. Regards, Harry

He clicked Send.

The ability to discover their current location from the cabin Harry had just discovered. One of the TV channels displayed something between a map and an aerial photograph, on which a bright orange symbol indicated not only their location but also the heading of the vessel. Another channel he fell across showed the schedule for the day's activities – which came as another surprise, since he'd forgotten there were any. His attention was drawn by one due to begin in ten minutes.

*

The lecture hall was a little larger than Harry expected – and a lot fuller. Sited on Deck Five forward, it felt perilously close to the coffee lounge but the sound of Spanish being spoken on the back row told him his erstwhile interrogators were not in these seats at least, and so, just as the lights went down, he slipped quietly into the only one spare.

One of the two check-shirted 'expedition' team members who stood in the spotlight on the podium announced that a French version of the talk would follow in half an hour, before introducing the speaker for the English-language version, a woman much younger than most expected but who exuded confidence by the barrel load. The slide on the screen behind her read 'Early Arrivals in the Empty

Continent'.

'We're following in the wake of some of my heroes,' she began in fluent English tinged with a distinctly German accent. 'Literally. Although the famous English navigator Captain James Cook [she pronounced his name 'Chames'] crossed the Antarctic Circle in 1773 – which is more than we may do in this voyage – he did not actually see the continent whose existence he suspected. It was to be almost fifty years before three ships from the northern hemisphere did so in the same year. That year was 1820 and they were captained by an Irishman, an American and a German. No, this is not a choke. [Laughter.] The Irishman, who served in the British Royal Navy, was the man after whom the stretch of water we are soon to enter was named. This is the Bransfield Strait and he of course was Captain Stephen Strait. [More laughter.] That *was* a choke. No, it was Captain Edward Bransfield, skipper of the English merchant ship, the *Williams*.'

Despite her youthful looks – or perhaps because of them – she held the audience in the palm of her hand. As she spoke, an image of each explorer and each vessel made a timely appearance on the screen behind her. Very professional, thought Harry. Twenty minutes passed very quickly, at the end of which she invited questions. The first of these came from a familiar voice down on the front row:

'I guess we all admire these explorers, like you do, but do you ever wish the continent of Antarctica had never been discovered?' It was Lennox.

For the first time, the speaker seemed slightly ill at ease. She recovered quickly.

'An interesting question I have never been asked. I suppose you refer to the environmental damage brought here by mankind and I suggest you ask the same question to my colleague Ralph, who will give a talk on that subject later in the voyage. Are you here, Ralph?

[No response.] Well, for me, I am very happy Antarctica was discovered, as it is... I think you call it a *barometer* for the world's climate. And it has also given me a job that I love very much.'

After a few more minutes, as the session closed and the audience began to disperse, Harry turned to the man sitting next to him. He'd practised a few questions in his head.

'*¿Es español Usted?*' he asked. (Are you Spanish?)

'*Sí, de Córdoba.*'

They continued in Spanish.

'Are there no lectures in Spanish?' asked Harry.

'Unfortunately not.'

'What a shame. I'd hoped to practise my Spanish.'

'Why don't you join our Spanish-speaking group in the bar after dinner? Eight-thirty.'

As Harry left the room with a new spring in his step, the tannoy leapt into action. The Captain had given the all-clear for a landing on Deception Island later in the afternoon, an announcement that drew a ripple of cheers from around the ship. And the first to be called would be yellow glaciers and blue glaciers, followed by yellow icebergs and blue icebergs. To Harry this sounded very much like nonsense.

His Spanish being rather thin on Antarctic geographical terms, he veered away from his new friends towards Reception, where a young Filipino advised him to examine the small print on his cabin card. Apparently he'd been allocated to the Blue Icebergs. Striding back to his cabin to change for lunch, he found long-forgotten memories of school houses swimming back to his mind. As Harry closed the door, a young man who'd been following at a distance all the way from the lecture hall continued without hesitation along the corridor, but nevertheless made a mental note of the cabin number.

6

That afternoon

'Land ahoy!'

This time the call was right – and Vernon evidently took great pleasure in making it. Harry had found himself among the same group that had observed the icebergs that morning, on this occasion peering off the starboard bow from the crowded promenade deck that wrapped around Deck Six like a human necklace. Emerging from a misty horizon were not one but two landmasses.

'Nelson Island to the left,' announced Vernon with confidence, 'and Robert Island to the right. Nelson Island named after, er...'

'Nelson? Wild guess.' suggested Lennox.

Harry was warming to the American.

'Indeed. And Robert Island was named after...'

'A man called Robert?'

'A *boat* called Robert,' said Vernon, with a brief frown. 'A boat owned by a British sealer. Both are part of the South Shetland Islands.'

'Is it Antarctica?' asked Maisie.

'Technically... ' started Vernon, but whether it technically was or technically wasn't Harry didn't hang around to discover, taking the opportunity to duck out of the geography class and watch from the more spacious environment up on Deck Nine.

As *MS Sturlanga* manoeuvred between the islands through what a voice on the speakers identified as Nelson Strait, the passengers got their first close-up view of Antarctic territory, if not the continental land-mass itself. A silence fell over them. Free from snow except for a few sheltered gullies, both islands seemed to comprise just bare grey rock that had broken into scatterings of rubble on cold, empty beaches. No plants, no birds, nothing green, nothing moving. Harry wondered whether anyone had ever walked there. And even if they had, he pictured the centuries, even millennia, before any human even knew these places existed. Endless summers and winters, storm and calm had passed by here regardless of the follies of man. A whole continent, minding its own business, alone. Instantly, his life back home receded into a kind of dream. And so did the trivial irritations of the voyage so far. This was why he'd come here. Perspective. A reset.

The crackling tannoy broke the mood. It was the German voice.

'This is Stefan, your expedition leader. The Captain has given us the OK for a landing on Deception Island. Please wait until your group is called and then proceed to the waiting area on Deck Five midships. The first groups to be called will be...'

With some passengers immediately scuttling off, those remaining readjusted to get a better view. Located right in the middle of the Bransfield Strait between the South Shetland Islands and the outer islands of the Antarctic peninsula, Deception Island is a very strange place. From the air it wouldn't be difficult to make the right guess that it forms the rim of a giant volcano, the crater itself being filled with water. What would be less obvious is that it's still classed as active. As those on the decks of the *Sturlanga* stared at the gaunt, grey cliffs drifting silently past them, many wondered where they could possibly be planning to land. The cliffs clearly dived straight into the depths of the ocean. Little by little, though, a tiny gap in the crater's rim became visible, before opening out into a gap just wide enough to accommodate a cruise ship. Once inside the 'lagoon', the horizon widened to reveal a beach on the north side. As with every Antarctic landing from the *Sturlanga*, a small fleet of tenders – Zodiac inflatables in this case – would shuttle passengers from vessel to shore. Hence the schedule of landing groups.

Harry's Blue Icebergs being quite early in the list, he set off to get ready. Oddly, he felt simultaneously exhilarated and relaxed. The pre-cruise advice had recommended all manner of cold-weather items for the Antarctic climate: thermal vests, thermal pants, inner gloves, outer gloves, inner socks, outer socks, fleece hats, fleece coats... but so far the on-deck thermometer had barely dipped below zero. Milder than a January day in the Cotswolds, thought Harry. Nevertheless, the warning that anyone 'inappropriately attired' would be denied a landing sounded serious and so, after manoeuvring his body around the narrow cabin to squeeze into his thermals, he added a heavy sweater, water-resistant trousers, rubber boots, smart green waterproof coat and red life-jacket – the last three items supplied by the cruise line. Thus kitted out, Harry lumbered along the corridor to the waiting area feeling like a semi-civilised yeti.

*

Below the deck along which Harry walked, in the depths of Deck Three, a small team in just tee-shirts and shorts was busy lugging boxes, coils, cones and even small craft into position for despatch from the 'tender pit'. The cruise line to which *MS Sturlanga* belonged was a proud member of the International Association of Antarctica Tour Operators. All member organisations are required to ensure not only the safety of their passengers and crew but also the well-being of the local environment, its flora and fauna. To this end, no one setting foot on land that forms part of the Antarctic area is permitted to stray beyond agreed boundaries and – the sacred tenet of all such 'expeditions' – any location visited, be it land, sea or ice, should be left in the same state as it was found. Among the practical effects for the *MS Sturlanga* was that the first tender ashore should contain only crew-members, plus a veritable cornucopia of security equipment. Often the most surprising to passengers was the set of packs containing survival equipment – food, shelter, medical supplies – for the scores of passengers and crew who could, in the event of extreme weather for example, be stranded ashore for days. It wasn't only accommodation and shops that were absent ashore, but also any help for many miles around. In hostile conditions to boot.

Among the luggers was Heidi Bräutigam, the young German who'd given the morning's history lecture. Just twenty-five, she was already enjoying her third season in Antarctica and with each year had become ever more enthusiastic about her job.

'Here we go, Gisela,' she called to her colleague at the other end of a heavy yellow box, 'another month, another set of landings.' They were speaking German, after English the second lingua franca of the expedition crew – rather than the French used in passenger announcements for the benefit of the TV crew. 'Maybe we'll get some proper Antarctic weather this time.'

'I like it like this,' commented Gisela, just as young but slightly shorter and much less confident. She was one of several naturalists in the team. 'When I was tired of watching for albatross yesterday I even got in some sun-bathing.'

'At least you were outside. I don't get the guys that hide in the cabin all the time. To me!'

Gisela handed over a sturdy box with a red cross on the side.

'Like Ralph, you mean?'

'Exactly. You know what? I think he's swotting up yet more bad news to fill the head of that Benoit.'

'The TV man?'

'Yeah, and he's got plenty of empty space in there to fill up, believe me. One, two, three, pull!'

'You reckon? I think he's pretty cool.'

'Ha! So does he. Brain like a French croissant though. You wait till he interviews me – I'll put him straight on a few things. Especially any alarmist nonsense Ralph has fed him on climate change.'

'You're a sceptic?'

'I'm a realist, Gisela. Things happen, crap happens,' She grunted with effort between each phrase. 'Humans are bright enough to figure a way through it. At least some of us are. In any case, if Ralph Dulacki had his way, there'd be no more cruises and no more work for the likes of us.'

Realising that for Heidi this clinched the argument, Gisela had no come-back.

'All set for the oldies now?' she said.

'Sure thing,' said Heidi, hands on hips. 'Bring 'em on!'

*

Harry waddled into the waiting area just as the Yellow Icebergs were being called and so found all the spare seats in the process of occupation by his fellow Blue Icebergs. After less than a minute leaning against a pillar, he realised that, while his outfit may be appropriate for an Antarctic wilderness, it was anything but for the heated lounge of a floating hotel. Removing his gloves, he wondered how the others looked so cool.

'Looking forward to the landing?' asked his neighbour.

'Looking forward to getting outside,' he said.

An understatement. After the discomfort of Drake Passage, Harry felt a youthful eagerness for the new experiences such a remote land would bring.

Five minutes passed with no call. By now Harry had unzipped his coat, removed his hat and was energetically scraggling his hair. To distract himself from the heat, he pulled out his phone. Still on his 24-hour wi-fi voucher, he checked e-mails, saw one from Sami and clicked it. It was a scan of the solicitor's letter. The heading showed Hook and Tysoe to be located in Oxford. Ah yes, thought Harry, that's why he'd heard of them: some business or other from his student days. He began to read the letter.

Dear Mr Pound
I am acting on behalf of the executors of the late Louise Angela Kennet and would invite you to...

Harry's arm fell limp, dropping the phone with a clatter.

7

Instinctively Harry bent to pick up the machine, but found his face beside it on the floor. A hand under his arm, another grasping the phone which seemed to be moving away. The feel of a seat beneath his coat.

'He's fainted,' someone said.

'It's the heat,' said another. 'We should...'

But the tannoy drowned out this voice.

'Good afternoon. Would Blue Icebergs please now go to the disembarkation point on Deck Three. Thank you. *Bonjour. Les passagers avec...*'

'Come on, mate. You'll be better outside. Can you stand up?'

Harry wanted to say no, wanted desperately to get back to his cabin, but heard himself say: 'Yes, yes, I'm all right.'

His two helpers, whom he now saw to be two younger male passengers, lifted him up before one retrieved his hat and gloves while the other zipped up his coat.

'Come in the lift with us,' one said, while most of the other Blue Icebergs hurried down the stairs.

'The late?' mumbled Harry to himself as the lift jerked into motion. It must be another Louise.

'No, you're all right. We'll be on time.' It was the other helper. 'No rush.'

But Kennet was her surname. How many Louise Kennets did he know? And Angela? He didn't even know she had a middle name. Oh God, Louise, what's happened?

Own on Deck Three, as they walked round a corner into a long corridor, a welcome draught of cold air wafted into their faces. Shaking himself, Harry wondered how he could turn around, but they'd already joined a fast-moving, one-way queue. Ahead he could hear a regular beeping getting louder. Before he knew what was happening, a crew member with a hand-held scanner had beeped the cabin cards they'd all inserted into specially-placed pockets on their coat sleeves, first Helper One, then Harry, then Helper Two. Beep, beep beep. Suddenly in sight of a large dinghy bobbing on the choppy water, they joined another queue.

Maybe Louise's mother was also called Louise. What did the rest of the message say? He felt his pocket for the phone.

'Your phone?' said Helper Two behind.

'Er...' said Harry.

'Other pocket.' Harry felt it. 'I think it's OK.'

Someone in a red coat was beckoning them on. The expedition crew, formerly seen only in check shirts, now all sported red versions of the passengers' bright green waterproofs. He was saying something about disinfectant. Like two-legged sheep they were herded through a shallow trough that covered the soles of their boots with a grey, soapy liquid.

'What's happening?' Harry had spoken his disorientated thought out loud. Red Coat seemed concerned.

'It's OK,' said Helper One, 'he's with us. You're OK, Hieronymus.' Had he told them his name? 'Just put your feet where they tell you and you'll be in the Zodiac in no time.'

'Zodiac?' said Harry.

'Dinghy,' whispered Helper One, passing Harry's arm to another

Red Coat.

As two new hands twisted his body first one way and then the other, he slipped and landed bottom-first in the body of the Zodiac. Helper Two, who'd stepped beside him, lifted Harry up onto a space in the bench.

'There you go, old man,' he said. 'Hold onto this rope. You'll be fine on dry land.' And with this, an engine revved up and they bumped away from the vessel.

Old man? Not even as old as Louise. What was she? Early fifties? They didn't do birthdays.

From the dinghy the *Sturlanga* loomed above them like a floating skyscraper until heads turned towards land, where the preceding Zodiac, now empty, was powering away from the beach. Antarctica's lack of quaysides and jetties, except at some scientific and military bases, not only means all landings are by tender but also that some landings are into the water. Deception Island was one such. By the time Harry was swinging his boots over the edge of the dinghy and into the crystal waters of the Southern Ocean, his head was clearing. Brushing away more offers of assistance, he managed to wade his way to the beach and then across a few yards of small shattered rocks without further incident. After his two dedicated helpers had at last reassured themselves he was steady on his feet, they joined the rest marching off down the beach to the left, where – bizarrely – steam could be seen rising against a dark grey sky. Harry asked the nearest Red Coat if it was OK to turn right, where he'd spotted a largish, isolated rock emerging from the beach.

'Sure', she said. 'But please don't go beyond the cone, sir.'

A minute's noisy trudge later, Hieronymus Pound slumped onto the ground, leaned his back against the rock, pulled off his hat and, on a desolate island thousands of miles from home, put his head in hands. The tears that came were the first for many years.

*

'Eckshow!'

Even mangled by a French accent, 'Action!' is universally understood. The speaker was one of two men in green coats standing with their backs to the sea way beyond Harry's hearing. Action Man supported a heavy video camera on his shoulder, while his colleague held a long pole, at the end of which hung a fur-covered microphone. Facing them, higher up the beach, were one Red Coat and another Green Coat, the tallest of the four. After a much-practised smile, the latter began speaking to camera in French.

'Messieurs-dames, nous sommes enfin sur la terre ferme...'

It had been explained to his interviewee, an American, that all dialogue would later be sub-titled, French to English and vice versa. Green Coat eventually switched to English, featuring an accent even heavier than his cameraman's.

'Doctor Dulacki, you are a femous cleematoligist who 'as spent many years studying the cleemate of Antarctica. What is the situation 'ere at the very northern tip of the continent?'

Ralph Dulacki, middle-aged with short hair, narrow spectacles and, incongruous in his outdoor gear, a black tie, turned from camera to interviewer with the confidence of someone who'd done this a hundred times.

'Well, Benoit, I'm not sure I'm famous – yet – and actually we're not quite on the Antarctic continent yet either...

'Curt!' said Benoit, dropping his smile. The crew lowered their equipment as Benoit lowered his voice. 'OK, Ralph, you tell me what I should say.'

The two spoke quietly for a minute or two before Benoit gave the cameraman a nod.

'Tek two. Eckshow!' came the call.

Professional smile, *Messieurs-dames...* 'Doctor Dulacki, you are a respected climatologist who 'as spent many years studying the climate of Antarctica. What is the situation 'ere in the South Shetland Islands, just off the northern tip of the continent?'

'Well, Ralph,' he said, 'it's getting ever more serious. Since the 1950s the winter air hereabouts has warmed up by more than ten degrees Fahrenheit – over five degrees Celsius. That's a huge amount. To give you an idea of the impact, the ice-free season in the Antarctic Peninsula, which is about two hundred miles over there...' He pointed beyond the camera. '... lasts some ninety days longer than it did even earlier in my lifetime. Imagine summer in Paris lasting till Christmas.'

'*Incroyable.* Our viewers can get some idea of the impact of climate change from an amazing scene in front of us.'

On cue, the cameraman slowly panned round to show half a dozen people of various ages, shapes and sizes, stripped to their swimwear and frolicking in the shallow waters just off the beach. The crew member allocated to ensure the safety of these passengers, encouraged to take a dip in the Southern Ocean for the sake of a certificate, was the first in, but by now she'd emerged and was standing nearer the TV crew in her bikini, body steaming, eyes staring into the camera lens. It was not Ursula Andress. It was Heidi.

She had not escaped the gaze of Benoit Girault. After a long pause he spoke over the footage.

'*Ah oui. Tout un spectacle.* Quite a sight.'

*

Oblivious to all this in his solitary outpost, Harry sighed before gathering enough courage to look once again at his phone. The scanned letter was still displayed.

Dear Mr Pound
I am acting on behalf of the executors of the late Louise Angela Kennet and would invite you to contact me regarding a small bequest. The family

has asked me to be the main point of contact in these matters and I would therefore ask you not to contact them directly at this sad time.
I am usually available during normal office hours.
Thank you.
Yours sincerely
Bertrand Tysoe

Ironic, thought Harry. Not only had he never contacted Louise's family, but also known nothing of them, address or otherwise, except that they existed. Likewise, Louise knew very little of his own personal history, except for his being single and without close family. Their many conversations, mostly via e-mail but occasionally – preciously – face to face, would touch on their personal life just to back up an argument. And only then, remembered Harry, in desperation when faced with overwhelming evidence of the contrary case. He tapped his phone to find their last e-mails. No signal. Of course. Momentarily he'd forgotten where he was. What use do penguins have for mobile phones? Looking round for the first time since staggering ashore, he saw no penguins but plenty of humans, conspicuously colourful among the black and white wilderness – ah yes, Deception Island. There may be no wildlife, but he could see there was much activity among the green coats of his fellow passengers – one of whom seemed to be approaching him.

'Here you are like a lonely mermaid, Harry. You won't find a wife like that.'

Who else but Fiona? His mind mostly elsewhere, Harry was slow to respond.

'I doubt many mermaids are on the lookout for a wife,' he eventually managed. 'No Danielle?'

'Why is it people always say that? We're not attached at the hip, you know. She's off up the beach as soon as she sees that TV camera. Now, isn't this a desolate place? It reminds me of Tralee. Why do people come here, d'you think?'

Despite the many ripostes that crossed Harry's mind – not least inquiring why she had come – he wasn't in the mood and quickly saw a way out.

'I'm sure I don't know, Fiona. What I do know is I forgot to go to the loo before I came over, so I've got to catch the tender you came on to get back to the boat.'

'Ah, so that's why you're here – waiting for the next bus.' After he'd hauled himself to his feet, the two of them crunched their way back towards the waiting Zodiac. 'The Lord knows you'd be in trouble on that score pretty fast if you got stuck out here.'

Harry nodded as she set off after her friend, before adding: 'I'd imagine that'd be the least of your problems.'

8

Steadier on his feet than when he'd disembarked, Harry was nevertheless obliged, as everyone was, to accept a helping hand back aboard. After thirty seconds in the noisy boot-cleaning machine and a quick beep of the sleeve-bound cabin card to register his return, he at last got back to the solitude of his cabin, to a blissful escape from his excessively snug kit. Blissful in normal circumstances. Right now nothing seemed normal.

His first decision was to avoid dinner in the restaurant, with its inevitable enquiries as to his welfare, and instead pick up a takeaway from the little snack bar he'd noticed by the coffee machines, scuttling back to his cabin armed with sandwiches, fruit and wine. His second was to set about this while letting his mind return to Louise. The news still seemed unreal. He realised he didn't even know how he was supposed to react.

Harry Pound felt that in his forty-plus years he'd had more than his fair share of death – mother, father, brother and only recently his favourite uncle. Despite an outward pretence of robustness, he was objective enough to know that each had affected him profoundly. In the case of the first three, he also recognised that his active avoidance of romantic entanglements was at least in part down to their cumulative effect – if losing someone close is so much of a trauma, why set yourself up for more? It was another matter with friends, though, wasn't it? They'd come and go, but an irrational part of him assumed they'd still be there somewhere, even if he wasn't – still in that corner of the pub, still at the same old parties – for ever.

Louise, however, had been different. The fact that, after the first few months, their relationship had been entirely platonic – indeed almost entirely *electr*onic – didn't detract from its importance to him. Even out of contact his thoughts had regularly turned to her, not just to construct an argument she'd delight in destroying, but simply to wonder what she was doing, where she was. That was both the beauty and the frustration of e-mails: the other side of the conversation could be taking place anywhere – on a different continent or, for all he knew, in the next room.

Pouring another glass of Malbec, he held it up against the port hole, watching the snow-streaked slopes of Deception Island dance in the red swell. When had he last actually seen Louise? Yes, that autumn evening at the Falkland Arms – they shared a bottle of red there too, probably putting them both over the limit. No, definitely. Was it worth the risk? Yes, definitely. Each venue was always her choice, Harry assuming it might be awkward for her in some places. After all, he never knew whether or not she'd told her husband about their rendezvous – or even about his existence – and she was well enough known in Oxford for the city to be out of the question. They'd talked of upcoming holidays – hers in the Spain with the family, his somewhere different for a change but, as ever, alone of course. He was sure he'd e-mailed her about the Antarctic cruise, but just to check he tapped on his phone to open the archives. As he saw page after page of messages from 'Sender: Louise Kennet', Harry's legs seemed to give way again and he just managed to steady the wine glass as he slumped onto the bed.

Head hung low over his chest, he once again sensed energy draining from his limbs. Action, he thought. He must *do* something.

Transferring to the small desk, he started tapping into the phone.

Dear Mr Tysoe
Thank you for your letter regarding my friend Louise Kennet. I'm currently out of the country for a couple of weeks and will make contact on my return.
It came as a shock to read of Louise's death, of which I hadn't been aware. Perhaps you could tell me a little of the circumstances – although I'd understand if this were not possible.
Kind regards
H. Pound

Having pressed Send, he immediately began composing a second message, this time to Sami.

Dear Sami
Thank you for the scanned letter. I wonder if you could do me a favour, as you're much better at these things than me? Could you please search the internet for any details of the recent death of a Louise Angela Kennet of Oxfordshire, aged about fifty-four. Ill health? Accident?
On business matters...

Firing off a few words of advice to his loyal colleague on a subject other than Louise seemed to clear his mind. Feeling the ship's engines start up reminded him where he was – and how long he must have been daydreaming. He swung round to flick on the TV. There was the bow camera showing the *Sturlanga*'s view of the narrow exit from Deception Island's sheltered lagoon. The next channel was yet another he hadn't noticed before: a video of passengers boarding this very vessel, the caption explaining that it was taken in Ushuaia just two days ago. Harry leaned forward. Yes, there it was: a straw hat, under which a tallish man was peering at his phone. No doubt checking the latest score from Cape Town. Harry felt an inexplicable urge to track this man down: here in a strange place in strange circumstances, he needed to talk with someone who was just, well, normal. Before he could locate himself on the footage, the camera panned away to focus on more passengers disgorging from the buses. That looked like Fiona and Danielle, both in floppy hats. And that... oh... now it had jumped to people in green coats. A caption briefly appeared announcing '*Girault en l'Antarctique, avec l'aimable autorisation de Canal Plus*'. Recognising both the presenter as the French alpha male from the bar and the location as the beach on which he'd been sitting only a short time before, Harry sat back to watch. This was excellent therapy, he decided, being nothing to do with Louise. He poured himself another glass...

*

Awaking with a start, Harry was relieved to see the glass safely – and emptily – sitting on the desk. His watch told him he'd dozed off for about an hour. The video channel, probably on a loop, had moved on to an interview on the open deck, in which both parties were well wrapped up in their coats, hoods flapping in the breeze, microphones close to their mouths. Something kept Harry from switching off – the intensity of expression on the face of the German girl he recognised from the lecture.

'He might have fooled you, Benoit,' she was saying in English. 'Where you and Ralph were standing was one of the mildest places in the Antarctic region. Not only is the Antarctic Peninsula itself the northernmost tip of the continent, but the South Shetland Islands are further north still. Sixty-two degrees south. The equivalent latitude of Bergen in Norway.'

'But in the northern hemisphere, there's surely the – what do you call it? – the stream of...'

'The Gulf Stream, yes. But where you were standing was actually in the crater of an active volcano that last erupted in living memory. Easily in living memory. No wonder it's warm. Didn't you see me in my bikini?'

'*Ah, oui*, Heidi. Indeed...'

'What I'm saying is the whole of Antarctica still has extremely low temperatures. We aren't even there yet. It's still the coldest place on planet Earth.'

'But your colleague Ralph told us....'

'Ha! Ralph Dulacki tells people many things.' There was no hiding her disdain.

'Are you saying his statistics are untrue?' Benoit Girault was sensing a controversy that would play out well on French TV.

'I'm saying his interpretation is biased. He's a well-known alarmist.'

'Per'aps we could arrange a live debate between you two?'

Although the hood flapped in front of her face, Heidi held the gaze of the tall Frenchman with her intense blue eyes.

'Bring it on,' she said.

Harry finally clicked the TV off with a thought that brought a smile to his lips: Louise would have loved this.

*

Harry wasn't the only one watching this channel.

Captain Ulrika Thommessen's cabin was remarkably spacious, unnecessarily so in her opinion, but then while most skippers of the line travelled with their families, she was single. It was supposed to be a sanctuary, a retreat from the pressures of the job, but on a normal voyage she found no need of escape from the job she loved. Nor did she make much use of her small office, just aft of the bridge. An enthusiastic devotee of 'managing by walking about', Captain Thommessen's home territory was the whole of the *MS Sturlanga*, where she could speak – and more importantly listen – to her crew in their place of work, and where passengers and crew alike could approach her with their comments, concerns and even the odd word of praise.

This voyage, however, was turning out to be far from normal.

Bizarre instructions from above received just before departure, a man overboard – and now this. She clicked off the TV, threw the remote on the bed, picked up the internal phone and punched in a number.

'Get the Frenchman to my office immediately.' She spoke in a steady monotone. 'Yes, Girault. And then have Stefan stand by. Is he indeed? Well, interrupt him.'

*

A slight swell gently rocked the *Sturlanga* as it approached the Palmer Archipelago, a group of islands running parallel to the Antarctic Peninsula itself. Most passengers prepared to brave the chill evening breeze were gathered on Deck Six forward, where a certain ex-geography teacher was expounding on the times of sunset within a month of the equinox to anyone who'd listen. Harry was not among them.

After a late coffee in the Polar Bar, he'd walked out across the open deck all the way to the stern, where he leaned on the rail, letting the hypnotic sight of the ship's wake consume his attention. It was probably because of his trance-like state that he didn't notice the young man join him, a few metres to his left. Until he spoke.

'*¿Habla español, señor, no?*'

Standing straight with surprise, Harry turned to face his neighbour, taking in his short stature, hunched shoulders, woolly hat and – evident even in the fading light – his sun-tanned features.

'*Sí, un poquito*,' he said. '*Pero soy inglés.*' He suddenly realised he'd forgotten the Spanish group. This must be one of them. But the young man continued in passable English.

'I speak a little English also. I looked for you at the Spanish group in the bar.'

'Ah yes, I'm sorry. Had things to do. Is it a friendly group?'

'This I know not, *señor*. I am not a member. But I know also that you have helped the Captain and the Security Officer in a matter –

how you say? – sensible?'

'Sensitive,' suggested Harry. Had this man been following him?

'Yes, a sensitive matter. And that you are connected perhaps to the police in England?'

With this, Harry's hackles were definitely raised. This man had been eavesdropping too. Steadying himself against the rising swell, he turned to face him as the young man held up both hands in an apparent gesture of appeasement.

'Yes, I admit it, Mr Pound, sir. I have given attention to you. And please believe me it is for a good purpose. I am myself a policeman.'

Harry looked sceptical.

'At this point, I should show to you my police ID card. But I have to say I do not carry it here. And this also is for a good purpose. I can however tell you my name.' He held out his hand. 'I am Clemente. Clemente Gil.'

PART

TWO

CONTACT

9

Harry accepted Clemente's hand, albeit with more than a little reservation. This Spaniard – yes, he didn't sound Latin American, but then neither did the accent register as being from those parts of Spain he was familiar with – this Spaniard admitted he'd been following him around the ship and failed to back up his claim of being in the police with any proof. And all 'for a good purpose', whatever that meant.

'Perhaps you'd better explain yourself somewhere in the warm,' suggested Harry, tilting his head towards the distant lights of the bar.

'I would like to do that,' said Clemente, 'for I too am feeling the coldness out here. I'm from Andalucía, in the southern part of Spain.'

'I know where Andalucía is.'

'Of course. I'm sorry. I'm nervious to tell you why I speak to you, sir.'

'Nervous,' corrected Harry.

'Yes. I'm also nervous that someone may hear us inside. I'm nervous that we should not be seen together.'

'Are you in danger?'

'I have been in danger for many months, *señor*. I do not want you to join me in this danger. But I do want to ask for your help.'

A silence fell between the men. A bird called in the distance. The spray from a sudden lurch against the waves swept across the deck and they both turned their backs to the sea. From nowhere a comment of Louise's came into Harry's head. 'You avoid people too much, Harry,' she'd said, 'except when they need your help – and then you stick to them like glue. It's a rare trait and a good one'.

'If you can explain yourself, I might help you,' he said eventually. 'But where? There's CCTV everywhere.'

'Except on the landings,' said Clemente.

Harry nodded. 'Of course. When's the next? Tomorrow morning?'

'At Damoy Point.'

'If you say so. But those tenders take us house by house.'

'House?'

'Group, whatever you call them. I'm a Blue Iceberg.'

'Ah, I'm a Green Avalanche.'

'Not sentences I ever expected to hear,' commented Harry.

*

Benoit Girault smoothed his hair, squeezed past the officer who'd led him to the Captain's office and entered.

'Ulrika,' he said, pulling back the chair beside the desk, 'how are you? So this is where you...'

'You won't be needing the chair, Monsieur Girault,' she said, remaining seated. 'This won't take long. When did you conduct the interview I've just watched?' He held out his hands. 'The one with Heidi Bräutigam.'

'Oh, two or three hours ago, I...'

'And whose approval did you seek before uploading it for broadcast?'

'Approval, Captain? There exists no process of approval. I...'

'There is now. You will consult my Security Officer before uploading any material. You will record no more interviews with my crew, neither the expedition crew nor the maritime crew nor the hospitality staff. And you will immediately remove this latest interview. When will your programme be broadcast on French television?'

'But some of it has already been broadcast, the embarkation in Ushuaia.' Captain Thommessen remained silent but her jaw muscles spoke volumes. 'It is all found in the contract with your company's legal...'

His voice drained away as the Captain rose to her feet.

'You fail to understand, Monsieur Girault. This is a vessel at sea. The only law here is maritime law – which, as far as you are concerned, means what I say *is* the law. You will no longer send material – videos, interviews, photographs, anything – to your television company during the voyage.'

'But...'

'Is that clear?'

'I cannot...'

'Is that *clear*, Monsieur Girault?'

'Yes, sir... er, madam.'

Captain Thommessen opened the door and stood back.

'*Bonsoir*,' she said without looking at her guest. 'Maria, send in Stefan, would you please?'

10

Next morning

'You sure there's a shop there, hun?' asked Maisie, peering through binoculars, shoulders hunched against the cold. The on-deck thermometer stood at minus three. 'You said there ain't none down here. All I can see's a coupla huts and the British flag. Union Jack, right?'

The safe paths for vessels of the *Sturlanga*'s size were now more restricted. In sailing south overnight between the islands of the Palmer Archipelago, they'd entered the Gerlache Strait, named after a Belgian explorer who himself had named the archipelago after the American sealer Nathaniel Palmer. Apart from a few evocative exceptions – Forbidden Plateau, Exasperation Inlet – the White Continent had for decades provided a blank canvas on which mariners chose to honour their heroes or patrons. By daybreak, which at this latitude in late summer came about six o'clock, the *Sturlanga* had gently negotiated the even tighter Neumeyer Channel and by the time some passengers were spilling out of breakfast and onto the open deck, she lay a few hundred metres off a headland of Wiencke Island named Damoy Point. Still low, the sun had turned the snowfields that spread between between grey-toothed peaks and ice-speckled water into a patchwork of black and white. As shadows shrank, a few isolated man-made structures came into view just above the waterline, with the cracked, grey face of a lumbering glacier for a background.

'Technically it's the Union *flag*,' corrected Vernon.

'I thought that was the Stars and Stripes.'

'There are other unions. In fact...'

'Post Office,' interrupted Lennox. 'They may sell stuff other than stamps.'

'You mean,' said Maisie, 'even though you can e-mail anybody from anywhere, the Brits who live in these parts still write letters home?'

'Postcards,' said Vernon. 'It's the postmark, you see. Some people – I mean cruise passengers like us – send themselves a postcard just for the franking.'

'You don't say? You guys sure are crazy. Hey, is it just me or is there a foul smell around here?' She eyed each of them before returning to the glasses. 'Wait! People. I can see movement near the flag. Two or three of 'em. Lots of 'em.'

Through the mysterious acoustics of American voices, Maisie's had carried some way along the deck and all eyes now turned towards the rocky knoll where the fluttering colours easily stood out from the monochrome landscape.

'Penguins,' said one young woman, 'Not people.'

'And I think,' said another, 'there may be some connection between what we see and what we smell.'

'Penguins smell bad?' asked Maisie.

'They didn't mention it in the wildlife lecture,' said Lennox. 'Which reminds me: we'd better get down to the climate lecture by that American professor. After last night's video, it'll be pretty full. Fi and Dani said they were going straight there.'

*

With a capacity for less than half the five hundred paying passengers, it was standing room only in the lecture theatre when Lennox, Maisie and Vernon arrived. Vernon just caught a glimpse of Fiona and Danielle down on the front row. There was no sign of Harry. After checking his first few slides, Dr Ralph Dulacki stepped up to the lectern. Even before he spoke, his short-sleeved, open-necked shirt seemed to make a statement on the subject in hand. Narrow spectacles emphasised a high forehead, which shone beneath short hair neatly combed around a side parting. He didn't smile.

'We arrive in Antarctica at a moment of crisis,' he began, without the introductory small talk favoured by fellow lecturers. Any residual murmuring died away. 'I said the same last year. And the year before that. What I have to say is not news. The Antarctic Peninsula is one of the fastest-warming places on Earth. Those of you who've been on deck this morning may have noticed a drop in temperature from yesterday, but that's just weather. And weather is not climate. This map shows the average temperature change in different parts of the continent over the last forty years. Red means warming, blue means cooling.' He paused while those who could see silently absorbed information from the big screen. 'Do you see any blue?' Heads shook. 'There isn't any. The darker the red, the greater the warming. You see this dark red area here?' Heads nodded. 'That's where we are right now. We are at the very epicentre of global warming, in the sense both of its impact right here on the peninsula and of the role of Antarctica in general as a barometer – a lightning rod if you will – for the deadly impact on our planet as a whole.'

Another pregnant pause. Lennox, who had a good view of the professor from the corner of the hall, noticed that he used no notes. He must have given this lecture many times, he thought. While Dr Dulacki's gaze passed silently across his audience, he suddenly spoke again.

'And we are responsible. You, me, your friends and family back home. We're all products of – and producers of – this dramatic rise in global temperatures over the last half-century. The power consumed by this ship to transport so few people – yes, so few – over such distances would have been unimaginable when many of us were born. You've probably heard some claiming there's no drama at all, no significant warming, no crisis.' Most of those present knew one such. 'Well, let me show you the truth.'

A series of slides followed, each reinforcing the case with clear diagrams representing clear statistics. The sources used were just as clear. Dr Dulacki invited anyone to meet him in the ship's library where he would show them these sources. The message was relentless. The professor was relentless. After twenty minutes of his half-hour slot, he summed up.

'I've shown you what is happening to our planet's climate. I've shown you why Antarctica is crucial – and will be crucial – in this process. Ninety percent of the Earth's glacial ice is here, remember. Those of you landing today on Wienke Island will see a small corner of it. In my next lecture in a few days' time I'll show you some critical results of this process and hope to discuss with you what might be done – that is, if it's not too late. Questions?'

The barked invitation was so sudden that for a few seconds the entire audience remained in stunned silence. Eventually a hand went up in the middle of the auditorium. The question asked by a middle-aged Scotsman was the one many had been pondering.

'Dr Dulacki, in a video interview yesterday one of your colleagues cast doubt on some of your conclusions and even on some of your statistics. Is there anything in what she said?'

The answer was not one any had been expecting.

'Captain Thommessen has asked me to stick to my own presentation.'

A muttering passed through the hall.

'And not to defend it?' asked the questioner.

'Exactly. Next question.'

After a few items on different types of ice, the speed of glaciers and the South Pole, the session concluded. Even while the applause died down, individuals formed a scrum at the front in an attempt to raise issues out of the spotlight. Stefan, the Expedition Team Leader, did his best to keep control. Lennox was not the only one to notice the absence of any other member of the expedition team. In fact the one he'd hoped would be there was already about half a kilometre away, approaching the rocky shoreline of Damoy Point.

*

'Are we on cones?' Heidi asked Gisela, as the Zodiac's motor died. While team members switched jobs between landings so they could fill in for absences, pairings were maintained unless there was any issue.

'You know we are. Stefan went through it.' She looked across the pile of equipment to her friend. 'Look, what's up, Heidi? You've hardly spoken a word.'

Swinging her legs over the side and dropping into the shallow, icy water, Heidi leaned on the tender with her elbows as she looked round the side of the bright yellow packets.

'I've been banned,' she said.

'Banned? From what?'

'From my own lectures. Jimmy's going to do the second history one and someone else has got politics.'

'Why?'

'You mean you didn't see the video?'

'I saw you making eyes at Benoit.'

Heidi snorted.

'You never do listen to what I say, do you, Gisela? Anyway, he's all yours. I'm banned from speaking to any of the TV crew and, apart from social chit-chat, to any of the passengers.'

'Till when?'

'Till back in Ushuaia.' With much splashing, she pulled herself up onto the rocks and took the rope. 'Or till I sort something out.'

11

Three hours later

On landing, all first-timers wrinkled their noses at the ever-present smell of droppings. Before long though they'd warm to the little characters responsible: scores of Gentoo penguins, none reaching higher than the thighs of their human visitors. After taking the obligatory photos, and holding the obligatory conversation with the cutest among them, most of the passengers trudged off with the help of walking poles along the line of red cones that led up the snow-covered slope to a low saddle, where the view was said to be best and from where the Post Office hut was accessible. Most, but not all. At the bottom of the slope, first one and then, just a minute later, a second turned left to a short stretch of bare, glacier-hewn rock facing north, away from the *Sturlanga*. Here the two men found boulders a few metres apart and sat down. Clemente's suggestion – that there'd be no problem in whichever of them was scheduled earlier asking to join a later landing party – turned out to be right. It was early afternoon and out of the wind the temperature had nudged up just a little.

'What a landscape,' said Harry, genuinely taken aback by the majesty of Anvers Island across the channel, where a mountain chain he hadn't even known existed rose straight from the sea like a rugged white giant to nearly three thousand metres, where it disappeared into the cloud layer. 'It doesn't look real, like the backdrop to a stage play.' Clemente didn't respond. 'Sorry, we don't know how much time we've got. We're out of earshot here, unless you think this little black-and-white chap is a spy.'

After a morning spent in thoughts of Louise, Harry had succeeded in placing that subject in a mental box that he'd left on the boat – and now found himself in a better, fresher mood here in the middle of another world. It wasn't a mood that seemed to be shared by his fellow rock-sitter, who glanced without amusement at the lone penguin waddling towards the shore.

'You'd better tell me what this is all about, Clemente,' said Harry. 'In English, if that's OK?'

He nodded.

'I make a short story from a long one,' he began. 'My job is a police officer for UDYCO in Málaga, *el Unidad de Droga y Crimen Organizado*... In English, you say the Drug Squad.' Harry nodded. Without knowing it, Clemente had already gone halfway to getting Harry on his side. 'About a year ago, they asked for a volunteer to help our colleagues in Argentina, where comes from many of the drugs to Spain. They wanted the outside person who could appear as an Argentinian. I have the right accent. I volunteered. The job was to be under the covers...'

'Undercover.'

'Yes, undercover. The outsider becomes the insider and reveals the network, the methods. It is a dangerous job...'

Harry watched the penguin consider entering the water as Clemente gave a brief and yet alarming summary of his activities 'under the covers' in Buenos Aires. The policeman was careful not to mention any names, of either individuals or organisations. Training, as ever, was his watchword. Harry was beginning to wonder how the

Spaniard had ended up here on the *MS Sturlanga* when Clemente's tale reached the morning, less than a week before, when, in a dusty square in the city centre, a fellow policeman had called his name. During the account of what followed, Harry glanced with increasing admiration at the young man sitting on the boulder on the chilly shores of the Southern Ocean. When he got to the point where he'd crouched beside the garden shed in the Ushuaia suburbs, Harry noticed Clemente shivering.

'It's cold here now,' said Harry.

'I'm glad to have this coat,' said Clemente, fingering his standard green waterproof. 'They gave it to me free on the boat. My own clothes are for summer. The only clothes for buying in the little shop are very expensive. Norwegian, I think.'

'Look, people are going back to the Zodiac. We don't want them looking for us. We'll find somewhere on the boat to carry on.'

'OK. If we can.'

'But before we go back, tell me one thing, Clemente. Your job was dangerous enough in Spain. Why did you volunteer for something even more dangerous over here?'

Clemente looked at the ground.

'I didn't say why I joined the police. My little brother Enrique is one of the victims of these gangs. He died from an overdose when he was only sixteen. They found that the drugs, they came from Argentina.'

And with that, Harry knew he was now a hundred percent committed to help – whether wisely or not. Pushing themselves up from their rocks, they alarmed the penguin, who finally dived into the icy waters.

*

'All this way and it was shut,' said Maisie after her first gulp of wine. 'Can't say I ever expected to feel so disappointed I couldn't get into a darned mail office.'

The usual crowd had assembled at what had already become their regular table in the main bar after dinner, this time with Harry captured too.

'Did you go all the way down there?' asked Danielle.

'We sure did,' said Lennox. 'It was a great walk now I come to think of it. Who needs shops anyway?'

Maisie shot him the irritated glance he was after.

'Oh,' continued Danielle. 'Someone told us not to bother, didn't they, Fi? So we just got lots of shots of penguins. Videos too. Do you want a look?'

She was sitting next to Harry, who was a little taken aback by this sudden positive change in Danielle's demeanour, but he dutifully admired snap after snap of identical penguins from identical angles.

'Did you enjoy the landing, Fi?' asked Lennox, aware the one who usually dominated the conversation – and who invariably came out with what he took to be Irish wit – was simply staring at her glass.

'They stink,' she said, 'those penguins. That David Attenborough never mentions they stink, does he now? And they shit where they stand on the snow.'

'Technically,' said Vernon, already halfway down his beer, 'the discolouration is from a fungus. Gentoo penguins mostly defecate on the bare rock, where they congregate to lay their eggs.'

'Gee,' said Maisie, 'you Brits are pretty up front about all these bathroom activities...'

'I'm not British,' mumbled Fiona.

'OK, you Europeans. What matters is where am I goin' to buy some momentoes?'

'*Mem*entoes.' Vernon said what Harry kept politely to himself. 'Maybe tomorrow at the Chilean military base. They say there's an actual shop there.'

'Oh,' said Harry, now interested. 'We're landing at a military camp?'

Vernon, of course, had a map to hand. Carefully, shifting the glasses, he spread it on the table between himself and Harry.

'Here,' he said, pointing and squinting. 'González Videla Base on, what's it say, Paradise Bay.'

'And we're here, right?' checked Harry.

'Correct.'

'But that means we'll be going backwards. I mean back the way we came.'

'Also correct. Seems we're on a zig-zag course because we have to book ourselves in at each of these landings.'

'Why the hell would that be?' asked Lennox. 'Who else is there?'

'That's what I asked the ship's Navigation Officer when we were chatting in the map zone.'

'When he was trapped there with you, more like,' suggested Danielle.

'Other cruise ships,' continued Vernon, oblivious. 'Can't say I've seen one yet, but apparently these are pretty congested waters nowadays.'

And for once the master of the trivial, had said something of significance.

*

Before Harry and Clemente had clambered into separate Zodiacs for the short cruise back from Damoy Point to the ship, they'd agreed where and how to meet up again in relative anonymity: in the main bar with the Spanish group. So it was that Harry made his excuses and left Vernon and his map, crossed to the other side of the bar area, mentally switching languages en route.

After a relaxed hour chatting with the Spanish-speakers about their country, their language – and, much to Harry's protestations –

their praise of his fluency, the group finally broke up and, on cue, Clemente wandered over from the bar to take up the spare seat next to Harry, which he'd engineered to be the one in the shadow of a flight of stairs. To anyone glancing over – or indeed to any CCTV camera – they didn't even appear to be in conversation. Harry had queried such precautions as over-zealous and had proposed simply meeting in one of their cabins, but this Clemente flatly dismissed as putting them both in danger, the reasons to be made clear when he'd continue his tale. As Harry supped his beer, therefore, he was once again all ears.

'Can you hear me OK?' asked Clemente, turning away from Harry.

'No problem,' he replied, likewise seemingly uninterested in his neighbour. The rising babble from the other tables ensured no one else could possibly hear. Despite this slightly ridiculous James Bond-like behaviour, he managed to keep a straight face. 'Carry on.'

Recalling the moment he'd tapped his second coded message into his phone beside the shed, Clemente resumed his story.

'I sent my contact a message saying I needed immediate help to exit from Ushuaia. Nothing happened for many hours. Now that I knew my enemy, I could explore a little. I was figurin' out how to arrive safely across the border in Chile when finally I received a message. It told me to wait till the passengers start boarding the *MS Sturlanga* and then to stand by the sailing boat opposite. Someone would bring me documents and I must join the queue.'

Harry's mind immediately went back to the northerner walking away from his wife. No, that didn't make any sense. A Spanish spymaster from Lancashire? Clemente had taken a sip of his beer and was once again murmuring. Only now did Harry notice he was holding a phone to his ear. Very clever. Maybe he *was* James Bond.

'It happened like they said,' continued Clemente. 'The man who gave me an envelope walked away without a word back into town. The passengers did not carry their own big luggage, so I didn't look from a different place...'

'Out of place?' suggested Harry.

'Exactly. The only problem in the registration was the medical certificate. I had none. But after the doctor made a phone call, he just waved me go through. Someone on board knew who I was. And since that moment I have been here as another passenger on holiday, with my cabin, my ID card and my account. Except I have no luggage and no much clothes. Already I visit the laundry two times.'

A few moments of silence followed, during which Harry considered lending Clemente some clothes – until he remembered there was a good six inches between them. Suddenly the crucial missing information occurred to him and he turned to Clemente.

'What has your contact, your handler, told you to do at the end of the cruise?'

Clemente still faced away as he replied.

'Nothing,' he said. 'There are no cellphone signals here. Yes, I have learnt how to send SMS on wi-fi, but nothing has come back. Nothing. Maybe it doesn't work.'

'So when we get back to Ushuaia, couldn't you still get over to Chile?'

'I'm not sure I will reach the end of this cruise, my friend. Group 21 has contacts all over Argentina – I know, I have used them. Never have I needed a contact in Ushuaia, but I am surprised if there is not one. The girl who shot at me – for sure she has made contact. Until yesterday I was hoping they didn't see me joining this cruise.'

'What happened yesterday?'

'I am in the cabin, always I am in the cabin. So I watch TV and there is me.'

'You've been on TV?'

'You also probably. I hear people say the Frenchman's video has already been on TV in Europe. And so maybe also in Argentina. I must fear it is so. Does Group 21 have a contact on this ship? I must fear it is so.'

'Among the crew?'

'Who knows? Maybe even the Captain.'

'Oh surely not. The Captain must have given permission for you to board and anyway, what has a Norwegian...'

But suddenly Harry was aware he was talking to an empty seat. As two drinkers from the bar noisily sat themselves opposite, in listening distance, Clemente was already walking off. On the table in front of him Harry noticed a small piece of paper, which he hastily scooped up and read:

Deck 9. Same place. 15 minutes.

He must have had it ready if needed, thought Harry. A professional.

*

The *Sturlanga* was still anchored off Damoy Point as Harry hunched against the aft rail in the dark. Even with the warm gear he'd collected from the cabin, he still couldn't lower his shoulders in the chill night air. Remembering to bring a torch, he'd looked at the on-deck thermometer as he passed: minus five. Come on, Clemente. No one else is mad enough to be out here. Eventually he saw a short figure approaching, passing in and out of the light as it walked by the paraphernalia fixed to the deck.

Just as Harry turned back to the rail, a shot rang out.

Instinctively he fell into a crouch. And then spun round. On the floor beside a stack of sun loungers lay a figure.

Another shot.

Where were they coming from? The figure lay still. Not for long though. It pulled itself up to its feet and sprinted back toward midships. Harry didn't move, staying in shadow. Another figure emerged from beyond the funnel and, without looking in Harry's direction, ran after Clemente. At least Harry assumed it was Clemente.

All fell silent once again. Even the echo of the shots evaporated into the icy wastes.

A rope rattled in a sudden breeze. Harry lay motionless for a while longer. Finally, convinced no one else was around, he stood up and walked briskly across the deck and into the small bar, where he slumped onto a bar stool, hands on the bar. He noticed they were shaking.

'Brandy,' he grunted to the barman, the same who'd been on duty when Joseph Challinor had gone missing. Harry looked up at him. Smart in his white steward's jacket, he was a young man with a neat pony tail and even neater beard. 'The man who just came in,' continued Harry, '... I mean two men. Did you recognise them?'

'Just now?' said the barman.

'A few minutes ago.'

The barman looked around.

'No customers. I have been tidying. I'm sorry, sir, I was not watching.' His accent was Spanish. 'I think I heard the door open. You are shaking with the cold, sir. This drink, she warms you up.'

Between downing his brandy and staring at the zinc bar, Harry settled on what he must do and looked for a few seconds at the barman as he fussed about the bottles.

'I need to speak to the Security Officer,' he said.

*

Half an hour later Harry was sitting on the edge of his bed, reading the note he'd found pushed under the cabin door.

If you report the shooting, please do not mention me. Staying in my cabin. Here is my email address. C

Obvious, thought Harry. Why didn't we do that before?

It had been a short and efficient session with Nils. Harry had hoped the Security Officer would come to him, but he was summoned once again to the small meeting room on Deck Five. Thankfully the bar had been thinning out and the usual suspects seemed to have already turned in. On news of the shooting, a sudden alarm had filled the eyes of the young Norwegian and he and Harry soon found themselves out on deck with Nils' female assistant, trying and failing to locate evidence of the shots in the dark. With no more information to be extracted from Harry, Nils had sent him to his cabin with instructions to try and remember anything else while it was fresh in his mind. The one thing that had most interested the Security Officer was Harry's impression that the second figure had, in sub-zero conditions, been wearing no coat, but a short-sleeved shirt. A check shirt. Of the first figure, Harry said he knew and recognised nothing.

It was a lie.

12

Next morning, restaurant

'What do they mean: 'Closed for the safety of guests'?'

Over his fried bacon Lennox was asking Vernon about the sign beside the locked doors out onto Deck Nine.

'Ice on deck would be the usual thing,' he said, 'except...'

As he took a sip of coffee, this time it was Danielle who took the opportunity to forestall him.

'Except it's not that cold,' she said. 'Fi's gone to look at the thermometer on Deck Six. In fact...' She glanced at her watch '... I bet she can't find it. Maybe we're moored out of the wind this time.'

They all turned to look out of the port-side window. About a kilometre away a long, low, snow-free shoreline reached out from the sweeping white hills they'd already become used to. Near the hilly end of the lowland two or three black huts could be seen, one of which was entirely painted in the red, white and blue of the Chilean flag. Beyond this tiny settlement a short stretch of mirror-like water – whether lake or inlet wasn't clear – separated it from the crinkly white face of another huge glacier, hanging over the scene like a frozen sea monster.

'Deck Nine's open again, folks.' It was Maisie, returning from the buffet. 'Someone said by the fruit salad. The end's still closed with tape though, beyond the hot tub. Say, can we see the shops out there?'

Before anyone could answer, the loudspeaker crackled into life and all breakfast conversations petered out. It was the German expedition leader.

'Good mornink and welcome to Waterboat Point, where today's landinks will take you onto the González Videla research station, operated by the Chilean Navy. They have confirmed that they are very happy to welcome us ashore, where we may take a tour of their living quarters and visit their small shop for souvenirs. Before I tell you the schedule of landink groups, I have some very important information, for we are not the only visitors to Waterboat Point today.' Surprised glances among the breakfast guests. 'We understand that a large colony of penguins is already in occupation, many more than you saw yesterday, and some of them are young chicks. I must remind you to stay at all times at least one metre away from the penguins – and please remember that they do not know our human rules. So if they cross your path you must please stop and wait. Now, the first group today will be called at ten o'clock and will be...'

'We don't need to listen,' said Vernon. 'It's all on the TV as usual. Oh, have I said something wrong, Dani?'

'No,' she said, standing up. 'I'd better go and find what's happened to Fi.'

But as she set off Fiona herself hurried into the restaurant, neat curls unusually awry.

'Where've you been?' asked Danielle, sitting back down.

'Checking the temperature, dear, like you suggested,' she said, slightly out of breath as she plonked herself next to her friend.

'And it is?' asked Vernon.

'Oh, spot on zero. Not too bad, eh?'

'I knew it. Not as icy as yesterday. I'm off to see what's happening on Deck Nine.'

After staring at her empty place for a moment, Fiona seemed suddenly to realise she needed to collect some food and stood up again.

'Are you sure you're all right?' asked Danielle.

'Yes, yes, fine,' replied Fi. 'Never been better in fact.'

*

As his friends were taking breakfast, Harry was only just waking up after his late night and a disturbed sleep. His eye was caught by another note under the door, this time printed with the cruise line's official letterhead.

Dear Mr Pound

There have been some developments after last night's incident. I would be grateful if you could report to the meeting room on Deck 8 at 8.30 this evening, if convenient. In the meantime, I ask you not to mention details of the incident to fellow guests. We will make an announcement in due course.

Nils Bakke

Chief Security Officer

While not thrilled by the 'report to', Harry immediately knew he'd be there on the dot. A short walk to Deck Six's drinks machine gave him time to make a decision he'd been pondering anyway, before settling back in his cabin with coffee, smartphone and renewed resolution. First was an email to Clemente.

Hola C

I guess you're OK after last night. I reported the incident of course but no, I didn't mention you. I'm working on a plan to help you. Cannot explain on email. Please meet me by the lift on Deck Five at 8.15 tonight. It will be as safe as anywhere.

H

Tapping Send gave Harry the satisfaction that he was in control once again. After a gulp of coffee – as disgusting as ever – he turned to his inbox. No message from Hook and Tysoe, but one from Sami.

Dear Mr P

I hope your voyage continues satisfactorily. Everything is ship-shape also many miles from the sea here in Moreton.

> I attach below two articles I have discovered in relation to the death of Ms Kennet. As you will see, the second one is from a Spanish news site and I have not attempted to use the automatic translator, knowing that you are most skilled in this regard yourself.

> We have a MORAL DILEMMA. Your suggestion of a venue for lunch on Tour E07 'Spoils of Empire' was once the home of a gentleman whose spoils were gained largely in Barbados, the very home of most of our guests in this particular coach party. Might we be sailing into troubled waters?

I remain...

Yours sincerely,

S Khatri

The first attachment, from the Oxford Mail, was merely a formal announcement of the 'sad and sudden' death of Dr Louise Kennet while on holiday with her family in Spain on December 18th, plus brief details of her college and position. So she'd been dead for well over two months, thought Harry, deeply ashamed he'd not been in touch.

The second, however, was intriguing. It was from a local online newspaper in north-eastern Spain, revealing that the body of 'academic doctor Louise Kennet, of England's ancient Oxford University' had been found in a remote part of Cap de Creus. A local police chief told the newspaper she'd been reported missing by her family, but it was only twenty-four hours later that her body was found by a local walker. It was believed she'd died in a cycling accident. Harry got up and walked to the port-hole. Small icebergs floated slowly past, oblivious to the concerns of the world in general and humanity in particular. Three things mystified Harry. Horse-riding yes, but cycling? Harry had never even known Louise *could* cycle. She'd never mentioned it. And if she was on holiday with her family, why was she cycling on her own? Odder than all this, though, was the location. Jutting out into the Mediterranean just south of the French border, Cap de Creus was at the heart of the area where he himself had spent the best part of a decade living and working. Though she'd never visited of course, Louise knew where he'd lived. Had she booked a holiday there, surely she'd have mentioned it. They had no secrets. He shook his head. Well, perhaps they did.

All this, however, needed to be stored in a mental freezer until he got back. He had some urgent investigations to do here. In one of Louise's rare comments on his own life, she'd encouraged him to get away more, to take it easy. Well, he'd tried. Another had been to translate some of the 'admirable' moral stances he'd adopted in their debates into his own behaviour. Quickly sitting down again, he tapped out his reply to Sami.

Dear Sami,
Thank you for the information. As to the Barbadian connection, I chose this venue on purpose in order to bring this 'elephant in the room' out into the open. (I may have mixed my metaphors there.) PS One may remain 'an obedient servant' but not 'yours sincerely'. I'm afraid I don't know why.
Regards, Harry

Good. Up to date. Hunger called.

*

Having picked up some food from the buffet, Harry walked up to Deck Nine with the intention of re-taking last night's position by the rail to see if he could oblige Nils with any more details that might surface from his memory. Just as he caught sight of the security tape, he also spotted, standing behind a raised part of the deck, two men in conversation. One was Vernon and the other, in hi-vis jacket and gloves, appeared to be a crew member. Something about them made Harry stop in his tracks and turn away to lean on the starboard rail, out of sight – but not out of hearing. They were discussing the closed section of the deck.

'But there's not any ice at all, so far as I can see.'

'It can be dangerous anyway. Treacherous, I think is the word.'

'It all seems rather over the top, I must say.'

'I'm sorry, sir, I have orders. No one to pass for the moment.'

Slowly Harry realised what was odd. The man was surely Vernon – hatless, comb-over fighting a losing battle against the wind – but the voice was not. Gone was the rough Eastender, replaced by a country house accent: more Windsor than Whitechapel. Intrigued, he munched on his bacon sandwich while straining to peek round the corner. Yes, there were just the two of them and the Englishman was indeed none other than Vernon. Turning back to the view, without taking it in, Harry's eyes narrowed.

13

Deck Eight, that evening

A quiet corner behind the *Sturlanga*'s main bar was set aside as the 'Expedition Library'. In practice it was just a small collection of well-thumbed natural history guides, one or two geology text books and a noticeboard where sightings such as seals (many), whales (fewer) and albatross (just one) were posted. Always on hand was at least one of the expedition team. On this occasion it was Gisela, taking bookings for the next day's kayaking, and her boss Stefan, the expedition leader with film-star looks who'd given the day's lecture on Antarctic politics for those who'd not gone ashore. Dinner just completed, Danielle and Lennox perused the books, while Harry took up a position next in line for a question to the team. Ahead of him and already in interrogation mode was Fiona.

'It was chaos out there today,' she said accusingly to Stefan.

'I was not at today's landing myself, but I understand it was very popular', he said. Harry realised this was the owner of the soporific voice frequently heard on the speakers. 'Did you get to see what you wanted?'

'Not for me, for the poor little penguins. They were under constant attack from those terrible screwers.'

'Screwers?'

'Skewers?' suggested Harry.

'That's them,' agreed Fiona. 'They were dive-bombing the penguins, even the little babies. I tell you, one poor mother was actually dead right by our path and no one moved the body. Nobody lifted a finger, except to put one of them cones beside it, like some plastic headstone, God help the little bird.'

'Ah yes,' said Stefan, showing as much sympathy as he could muster. 'These things happen. I am sorry if you were upset, er, Fiona, but it is nature. We must not interfere.'

'Ah, you're probably right. Anyway, do you think tomorrow will be calmer, Steven? I hear there's another landing on the schedule.'

'Weather permitting, yes, madam.' It was Gisela who'd intervened. 'We'll be in Andvord Bay and there should be fewer passengers ashore because of the other activities. Can I interest you in the kayaks?'

She might as well have invited Fiona to a ceilidh in the Devil's kitchen.

'You cannot!' said Fiona. 'Can't you see my age?'

'What about you, sir?' suggested Gisela, smartly turning to Harry.

'I think not,' he said with a smile, 'but thank you anyway.' With Fiona now on her way to the bar, he carried on. 'My question is about other vessels, though. I hear other cruise ships are in the area. Do either of you know if we'll be seeing any?'

Stefan answered.

'It's possible, sir. In fact we're usually in the same area as our sister ship, the Grettis, somewhere around here. They're on their way back north. But in Antarctica cruise ships try to avoid each other – it lets our guests feel more isolated in the wilderness.' Harry felt Stefan was sharing a secret with him. He rather liked the genial German. 'If you like, I could find out and let you know. Where will you be later, sir?'

'In the bar till about eight-thirty. That would be excellent, thank you.'

Excellent, indeed, he thought. A plan was forming.

*

Joining Vernon and Maisie, who'd reserved their table in the bar, the six of them settled into what had become their regular resumé of the day.

'Now, Vernon, you're the man for this,' began Lennox. 'I can't get a definite answer from either maps or books: were we on the mainland of Antarctica today or not?'

'The answer's yes and no,' said Vernon. Harry noted his accent had migrated once more to the East End. 'Yes at low water, no at high water. In fact also yes in winter and no in summer. The naval base is on Waterboat Point, which is technically an island but I wandered as far as the cones let me – round the back of the hut – and a thin bridge of ice just connected it to the mainland. So today you could've set off to walk all the way to the South Pole.'

Fiona shivered.

'And I know a few mad enough to do it,' she said. 'Enough of these schoolboy fantasies. What about the shop? Now, Maisie, did you manage to buy anything today?'

'It weren't easy, I'm tellin' you,' said Maisie, 'unless you got some kinda tea-towel fetish or a mania for mugs. But, you know that cute young sailor persuaded me to...' Facing the rest of the bar, she was staring into the distance. She lowered her voice. 'Say, ain't that the English lady whose husband went overboard?'

All heads swivelled.

'It is,' said Harry, 'but we shouldn't...'

Fiona was already up and bustling, though.

'Looks like we already have,' said Lennox.

'... shouldn't stare, I was going to say.'

Whether willing or not, Karen Challinor found herself being firmly led to their table. Shorter than Harry had remembered and noticeably more frail, she still wore the same stern expression as when he'd last seen her with her husband in the Polar Bar. In short order Vernon found himself ejected from his seat by Fiona, now in full management mode, and despatched to the bar for a white wine.

'This is our little group, Karen,' she said, positively pressing her down onto the empty seat. 'You'll be less nervous here among us. I'll tell you our names even though you won't remember them.'

As Fiona gave an unnecessarily detailed resumé of each, Harry's mind went back four days to the chilly outside seat he'd occupied while this woman's husband was apparently meeting his doom. Distracted, he didn't see the barman approach, wheeling a rickety trolley to collect the empty glasses. Harry froze. He stared straight ahead. Someone was speaking to him.

'I said isn't it, Harry?'

He looked up.

'Sorry, what?'

'I was telling Karen your name's really longer than that, isn't it?'

'What? Yes.' He looked at his watch. 'Sorry, I've got a meeting. Vernon can have my seat.'

Watching him go, Fiona turned to Karen, who'd still not spoken.

'Well, I'd call that rude,' she said.

*

Harry had to wait by the lift for Clemente. When he eventually turned up, it was with eyes constantly darting about: ahead, behind, to the sides. Assuring him they'd be safe together, Harry led him first into the small shop, then out of its rear door and across to the meeting room without a glance into the bar. Captain Thommessen and Nils Bakke were waiting. Both rose as Harry introduced Clemente Gil, prompting the Security Officer to fetch another seat. Three had been crowded, four was cramped.

'Yes, we both know who Señor Gil is,' said the Captain, letting all sit before she did. While Clemente seemed both surprised and relieved by this, Harry was neither. Having checked that speaking in English was OK for Clemente, the senior officer turned to Harry. 'Mr Pound, you seem to be at the centre of every dangerous event on my ship.'

'By accident, I assure you,' he said.

'I expect you both have something to tell us, but may I first let Nils bring you up to date with what we've been doing ourselves?'

While his recent moment in the bar had added a vital item he wanted to bring up, Harry was happy to let Nils do his bit first.

'Yes,' he said, shuffling, avoiding his Captain's eye. 'First, in the daylight, we have found the two places where the bullets hit – and, finally, one of the bullets. It's not from any of the firearms we maintain for the safety of passengers on board and ashore. That is both a relief and a worry. That another lethal weapon has been brought aboard the *MS Sturlanga*, despite our strict security checks, is a serious matter. That two passengers have been put in danger even more serious.' Harry got the impression from Nils' flawless English that he'd practised this little speech. Throughout, Captain Thommessen examined Clemente. 'Given the observation of the perpetrator's shirt you shared with us, Harry, we have interviewed every member of the expedition crew to learn their location at the time of the incident. I have to tell you this has – I think you say it like this – this has not 'thrown up' any suspect. We must assume therefore that the perpetrator is still aboard somewhere and is still armed. Have you remembered any other detail, Harry?'

He shook his head.

'Sorry, no. Not on this incident at least.' Captain and Officer looked at each other and then back at Harry. 'I'll tell you later.'

'OK,' said the Captain, straightening up in a seat that was clearly too small for her ample hips. 'Now, let's be clear. Señor Gil, it's probable you were the intended target of these shots, am I right?' He nodded. 'I can guess why Mr Pound didn't share that with us last night.' Harry opened his mouth but her raised hand indicated he needn't bother. His thoughts briefly shot back to one or two interviews with his old headmaster. She'd turned back to Clemente. 'Are you injured in any way?' He shook his head. She once again adjusted her hindquarters before continuing.

'Now, in the early hours of the morning before our departure from Ushuaia, I received an urgent request from our head office in Oslo to accept a late, additional passenger. I'll tell you now I was reluctant. When the request changed to an instruction I was left with no choice. With no further information forthcoming, I simply informed my Security Officer here of the situation and instructed him to treat you as any other passenger. This we have done until today, when I further instructed him to have your cabin searched for a firearm when you were absent. Yours too, Mr Pound.' At this, both sat up straight. 'I make no apology for that. Nor for this.' She nodded at Nils, who gestured both men to stand up as he searched them.

'Thank you, gentlemen,' she went on. 'Our passengers' safety is our priority.' Harry's mind flitted to the catapult the headmaster had found under similar circumstances. 'Perhaps, Señor Gil, you might now oblige us with an explanation of why a last-minute passenger with no luggage has been put in our care.'

And so once again Clemente told his story. By the end, Captain Thommessen's attitude had softened, though not her determination. For a few moments she sat in silence. None of the three men dare speak.

'We must therefore assume, Clemente', she said steadily, looking at the floor, 'that someone from this Argentinian drug gang – or at least paid by them – is on board this ship and is intent on killing you. Whether passenger or crew we don't know – a check shirt, after all, is just a check shirt. Back at Ushuaia in a week's time – if, God willing, you make it that far – we must make sure you are met by a police escort. Is that a problem, Nils?'

'No,' he said. 'I've arranged it before.'

'But Group 21,' said Clemente, 'have contacts in the Argentinian police. I know it.'

'But anyway,' continued the Captain, 'do we want to spend a week with an armed gunman aboard, hunting down his prey? Are you sure it was a man, Mr Pound?'

'Not a hundred per cent.' said Harry.

'OK. Any suggestions?'

Harry opened his mouth, but Nils spoke first.

'González Videla?' he said.

'Hm, it's possible,' she said thoughtfully. 'But from Señor Gil's perspective, it is not really a solution.' He shook his head. 'We are just making his safe escape from Antarctica more uncertain by passing on the problem. And anyway, I am not the favourite visitor of Capitán de Santo. Our presence there is not always welcome.'

'I have another idea.' It was Harry. 'How do you get on with the Captain of the *MS Grettis*?'

Her face lightened.

'Go on,' she said.

'Well, I understand we'll be close to your sister ship tomorrow as she returns north – and she isn't headed for Ushuiaia but Punta Arenas, right? In Chile.'

'You're well informed, Mr Pound.'

'It's on the internet,' he said, shrugging modestly. Stefan had looked this up of course, but Harry let the inference that *he'd* researched it hang in the air. 'Are there physical transfers between the

110

ships?'

'Well, yes, there have been. Equipment and occasionally...'

'People?'

'In emergencies.'

'Which this is.'

Captain and Security Officer again exchanged a glance.

'We'll investigate it,' she said. 'We must speak with our Navigation Officer. In the meantime, Señor Gil, I'm not happy with you remaining in your cabin. The gunman must know it and has only stayed out because of the CCTV. I will make my own guest room ready. You will move there tonight.'

Clemente looked unsure.

'That's an instruction,' she said.

As they made to stand up, Harry spoke again.

'Er, I have something to add on another matter,' he said. They sat down again. 'In the case of the missing man...'

'Mr Challinor?' said Nils.

'Yes. You remember you asked me if I'd seen him return from the open deck?'

'Yes. You said you were ninety per cent sure you didn't.'

'Well, I still am. But I'm pretty sure – ninety per cent sure – I *heard* him.'

While this meant nothing to Clemente, the other two sat bolt upright, staring at the precise Englishman, who was now running his fingers through his shock of hair.

'Explain,' said Nils.

'Well, he had a limp, right? Everyone saw it but no one mentioned it. After he'd spoken those few words to me on the deck, I heard his irregular steps go off into the distance. I wasn't really paying attention – I didn't feel well, I may even have had my eyes closed – but a little later I remember hearing the same steps coming back and walking back through the doors.'

'Why didn't you mention this before?'

'Because we were talking about what I *saw*. I didn't remember any sounds until half an hour ago in the bar, when I heard a drinks trolley with a wonky wheel going past. I didn't see it, but I *heard* it.'

'Wonky?' asked Nils.

'Bent,' said the Captain. 'As in policemen.'

The reference was lost on Nils, who continued:

'So Mr Challinor came back inside.'

'Possibly,' said his boss, 'but it doesn't mean he didn't fall overboard somewhere else,' said the Captain.

'It makes it less likely though,' said Nils. 'It's more difficult on Deck Six. Thank you, Harry.'

'Yes,' said the Captain, standing up once more. 'Thank you, Mr Pound. You seem to make our lives both easier and more difficult. Quite a skill.'

14

Andvord Bay, the next morning

Even though the *MS Sturlanga* was equipped with advanced equipment for expedition cruises in the polar regions, sometimes the distribution of icebergs, large and small, is so dense that navigation by eye is still the safest method. Such was the situation that night in the Gerlache Strait and it was dawn before the order was finally given to weigh anchor and manoeuvre carefully away from Waterboat Point. It was a relatively short cruise, though, north then east then south-east and into the huge inlet known as Andvord Bay. The few passengers braving sub-zero temperatures on deck to witness their arrival were rewarded under clearing skies with a magnificent panorama. Nearly twenty kilometres long, Andvord Bay is a fjord. Unlike most of the fjords of Norway, however, the descendants of the glaciers that formed it are still all around. Arago, Rudolph, Bagshaw, Grubb – each stretches from the rugged, untouched peaks in a crazy kaleidoscope of whites and blues to form a sharp cliff face of ice looming over the still waters of the bay.

Still but not empty, for between the *Sturlanga* and the glaciers lay her sister ship, the *MS Grettis*. Still but not silent, for, as soon as the *Sturlanga* was safely anchored, from her tender pit a squadron of Zodiacs buzzed between ship and shore, laden with the usual bits and pieces to secure the landing and with the crew members to put them in place.

Among the handful of passengers outside on Deck Six was Harry, well wrapped up for what might be a long wait in the cold. Having chosen the promenade deck rather than open Deck Nine to observe the *Grettis*, which lay off the port bow, he'd been looking not at the scenery but at the stretch of ice-strewn water between the two cruise ships. In the middle of the night he'd been awoken twice by the ping of an email. Usually he'd switch his phone off while asleep, but it hadn't been a usual night. Both messages were from Clemente. The first confirmed he'd been transferred by Nils to the luxury of the Captain's guest cabin on Deck Eight. Of the Captain herself there was no sign, but he assumed hers was nearby. The second, sent at six o'clock, had – judging from its errors – been written in haste:

Trasfer aranged! Its soon. C

Harry replied:

Good luck! H

After this, there was no question of sleep. Surprised that his plan had been implemented so promptly – indeed, that it had been taken up at all – Harry had pulled on his gear and headed for the deck, where the sight of the *MS Grettis*, a virtual mirror image of the *Sturlanga* against the stunning backdrop of the Antarctic shore, had achieved what many supposedly emotional events in his life had not: brought a tear to the eye of Hieronymus Pound.

As soon as he heard the first tender rumble into life below, his attention was fixed on the water. And after just fifteen minutes, he saw what he'd been waiting for: a single Zodiac chugging not towards shore but away from it in the direction of the *Grettis*. His small binoculars picked out three figures, one in red, heavily padded in gloves and goggles at the wheel, another in red at the other end and, between them, sitting alone in the passenger space, gripping the rope as the little Zodiac bounced across the water before disappearing behind the *Grettis*, sat a short figure in green. It could have been anyone. But it had to be Clemente.

It was to be the last Harry saw of him.

*

'Would Green Snowdrifts please now go to the disembarkation point on Deck Three.'

'Would anyone who's booked a Zodiac cruise please assemble at the waiting area on Deck Four.'

'Would kayakers with a blue ticket please report to the main bar on Deck Eight.'

Cold as it was, in Antarctic terms it was a fine morning and the activities offered by the *MS Sturlanga* were at full throttle. Offered at a price, naturally. With no immediate tasks demanding his attention and finding, somewhat to his own surprise, that he'd come to terms with Louise's death – however mysterious – Harry signed up for a Zodiac cruise. While waiting with others on Deck Four, just along from his cabin, he noticed Nils passing by and silently raised is eyebrows. The Security Officer hesitated before giving Harry a definitive thumbs up. What he hoped he'd observed earlier must indeed have been the case. A further wave of relief came over him.

From the Zodiac he hoped to get a good look at the *Grettis* too. In this, however, he was to be disappointed, for, as he sat on the side of the inflatable, hands gripping the rope behind like he'd seen Clemente do, no second cruise ship was to be seen. It must have sailed away while he was having breakfast, leaving the paying passengers of the *Sturlanga* in their perceived isolation. In its place a seascape of broken ice spread out before them, apparently endless to the north, but closed in to the south by the most dramatic scenery Harry had ever encountered. Gone were the occasional tongues of bare rock reaching out to the waterline. Everything but the steepest slivers of high rock face was white. A brilliant, virgin white where no man can have stepped, where surely anyone would be just a tiny, insignificant speck, like a mouse on the moon. There were two crew members, the pilot and the guide, both even more tightly wrapped up than the passengers, since they might well be out here all day. The guide, a young woman in her twenties, drew their attention to rafts of penguins flipping in and out of the blue-grey waters, a leopard seal lounging on an iceberg, the distant spray that warned of a calving iceberg. Whenever she waved the pilot to cut the engines, an unstoppable torrent of camera clicks filled the silence. Harry's head spun this way and that. Photos weren't what he wanted – after all, who would he show them to? Memories were what he got. Along with, to his surprise, an overwhelming sense of wonder that he hadn't experienced for as long as he could remember.

After a quick lunch back on board, where none of his friends was to be seen, he was out again, as part of the scheduled landing for the Blue Icebergs. This time the landing area was entirely snow-covered and therefore penguin-free, which meant it was also cleaner – and fresher. Having been told they could have an hour ashore, the expedition crew started calling the dispersed passengers in after just thirty minutes, with the skies clouding over and light snowflakes drifting in on a freshening breeze. By the time their tender pulled up by the *Sturlanga*'s pontoon, the snow was falling thickly from a cloud level low enough to blot out most of the peaks. Harry wasn't the only one for whom a shower and a snooze in the warmth of his cabin were becoming an ever-more attractive prospect.

*

The main attraction of that evening's post-dinner bar session was the re-emergence of Benoit Girault and his acolytes, who'd been out and about for most of the day interviewing passengers as they experienced 'the best of the Antarctic', as the cruise line's marketing would have it. Chosen as his theme for anyone he could capture was another line that popped up frequently in their literature: the idea that every passenger would return home as an 'ambassador' for the white continent, promoting its protection by their elected representatives. As he muscled in on Harry's group, the notion got short shrift from Fiona:

'Oh, sure as I'm sitting here, that's been dreamt up by some whizz-kid in an office who doesn't want that Greta Thunberg and her friends banning the business that pays his rent.'

'Do you not agree with Greta then, Fiona?' he asked, holding his microphone between them like a shared ice cream. 'Is there no climate emergency?'

'How would I know that, young man? All I know is the little girl should be at her school desk.'

'What about you, sir?'

He'd turned to face Harry.

'You mean will I sing the praises of Antarctica to my friends at home?' said Harry.

'Well, will you?'

'I probably will. It's certainly a spectacular place. But you may be over-estimating us. I think I'm safe in saying that most of us here...' his gesture took in not just their group, but the whole bar. '... are not what people nowadays call influencers. We're a bit long in the tooth for that.'

'Long teeth?'

'Too old, *monsieur*. And even though back in England I live near some politicians and even royalty, my only connection with any of them might be to complain about Chelsea tractors parking on pavements.'

While this raised a laugh among his friends, it seemed to leave the Frenchman even more befuddled. Pretty smartly he moved on to the next table – a group of earnest-looking Germans who might take him more seriously. Irritated by his departure was Vernon, who had naturally prepared a whole tranche of information with which to dazzle the TV presenter and his audience. Given the number of beers he'd consumed after an active day outdoors, thought Harry, it was perhaps just as well Benoit had moved on.

Little by little the bar emptied, the bartenders cleared away the final glasses and all fell silent on Deck Eight as, apart from the night shift, all the crew and passengers of the *MS Sturlanga* retired to their cabins.

All except one. It wasn't only Clemente's cabin that remained empty that night. Another cabin on another deck failed to witness the return of its occupant. That night – or ever.

15

Next day, London

The taxi rank outside King's Cross station was busy as usual. Passengers bustled from their trains, scuttled to a cab and leapt in, while those leaping out seemed in even more of a hurry. Just one person stood motionless among the comings and goings.

It had been three and a half years now, but each time Josh Burnet came down to London since then he'd stood quietly here for a minute or two to remember. It was here that he'd seen his little brother Arthur for the last time. Well, the last time alive. While this was his personal ritual, the one next to Cook's memorial up at Ayton had been shared – even when, four days days ago, the sharing had been virtual and he'd sent a photo to prove he was there. He could give this one up when he wanted, but how long was the other one, with its little verse – a prayer really – destined to continue? For ever? He still missed Art, of course he did. But perhaps a parent's loss was greater than a sibling's. Who knows, he thought to himself and turned to take the steps down to the Tube. Art's taxi to Heathrow had been on expenses but, with the business running on a tight budget, for Josh it was the Piccadilly Line as usual up to Finsbury Park.

*

He turned the key in the door, pushed it open against a small pile of post, switched on the hall light and dropped his back-pack to the tiled floor. What would have seen as a rather run-down dive in most towns had become a multi-million-pound property purely because of its location, less than five miles from the City. His father's *pied à terre*, as he'd called it, had turned out to be an astonishing investment.

Josh's own investment in the café, while more modest, was looking good on turnover but not so healthy on profit. The appointment to try and address this wasn't till the morning and so, having done his other duties by checking out the state of the place, empty for two weeks, sending a three-word report ('All OK here') to its usual occupant, currently nine thousand miles away, and finally checking in with Paula, he slumped to the sofa with a glass of wine in front of him.

Next to the glass on the coffee table was a letter from the cruise line, detailing the likely itinerary. After a generous gulp of red, he put his feet up for a little browse. It wasn't just the schedule actually; it also listed some of the lectures and activities on offer. Flicking through, he was surprised by how many things there were to do. Eventually, he dropped the sheets back on the table, took another sip of wine and lay back to imagine what he might choose if, one day, he and Paula had the funds to set off on such an adventure.

Two minutes later, he sat bolt upright. As he grabbed at the letter again, the glass tumbled onto the carpet. Page one, page two... here it was: Experts in Their Field. Tracing his fingers down the page, he stabbed at one line.

'Oh no!' he shouted out loud and stood up, fully alert.

And worried.

16

Same day, MS Sturlanga

Once again the small lecture theatre was packed. With the *Sturlanga* cruising back up the Gerlache Strait to another inlet, the combination of no morning landings and the recent theme of the wandering Frenchman's sporadic interviews had brought an eager audience to Ralph Dulacki's second lecture on climate change. With five minutes to go, the equipment checks were being done not by Dr Dulacki but by Stefan, the expedition leader. After checking his watch, he left the podium and, squeezing through the audience, walked out of the back of the auditorium. Ten minutes had passed before his return, when he mounted the podium, hands gripping tightly to the lectern. The murmuring subsided.

'Good morning, ladies and gentlemen,' he began. The gentle voice was no more. 'Did you enjoy yesterday's activities?' A few cheers, plenty of impatient mumbles. 'Good, good. Well, we are well on the way to Charlotte Bay, another spectacular location where the Captain has told us we may manage one or two landings later this afternoon, but most will be tomorrow. This morning's lecture programme was due to start with the second of Dr Dulacki's popular talks on climate change, but I'm afraid he is... I think in English you say 'out of sorts'. I will let you know when this will take place. And so in one hour's time please return for our next scheduled presentation on Antarctic flora and fauna.'

Cue loud mumbling and a stampede for the coffee machine.

*

'Well, where is he?'

Captain Thommessen was standing, arms folded across her chest, on the bridge. Through a fan of windows the blue-and-white view slid slowly by, closely observed by one officer as his colleague moved between an array of computer screens, now and then calling out numbers. The Captain, though, stood with her back to all this. Tiring of the trials presented by an unusually troublesome voyage, she'd come to the place where she felt most at home, with her calm and reliable maritime crew. And now Nils had arrived with Stefan in tow and with yet another problem.

'Well, not in his cabin,' said Stefan. 'Nor has he slept there, it seems.'

'When was he last seen?'

'No one I've yet spoken to recalls seeing him since yesterday. But, as we all know, Ralph is not the most sociable in the team. He's also one of the few with a cabin to himself.'

'I repeat: when was he last seen?'

Nils took up the baton:

'He checked back aboard from the landing at Andvord Bay at 15:15. He was the only one with no duties yesterday. I encouraged him to be on hand at the library to generate interest for his lecture this morning, but Gisela tells me he didn't turn up. His cabin card wasn't used at the bar – or anywhere but the tender pit – all day.'

'Is he drunk somewhere?'

Both men shrugged. All crew members were strictly banned from alcohol consumption for the duration of the voyage. While the Captain was aware that some was probably smuggled aboard, she thought this improbable in Ralph's case and changed her tack.

'Or could he have spent the night in someone else's cabin and still be there?' she asked.

Both men now seemed taken aback.

'Well, he may not be the youngest crew member,' she went on, 'but he's not past it.'

'Extremely improbable, ma'am,' said Stefan, somewhat prudishly.

'Very well. If you agree, Nils, we should hold off making any announcements until we have no choice. We managed to keep silent on the shooting business. Stefan, organise systematic interviews of all your team: someone must have seen him somewhere. Ask about any strange behaviour. You know the drill.'

'Yes, Captain.'

'Nils, search his cabin. Phone, cabin card, outdoor clothing, that kind of thing. Then search every corner of the ship. He may just have collapsed in a corner.'

'Yes, Captain.'

As the two men left the bridge, Ulrika Thommessen swivelled round to take in the view over the bow once again. The morning's bright skies seemed to be clouding over. Snow was blowing off the icebergs like dandruff. Her thoughts turned involuntarily to the diligent Englishman. She hoped Mr Pound was not yet again 'accidentally' involved in this incident too. Or perhaps, she thought on reflection, she hoped he would be.

*

Half an hour later, in the echoey vaults of Deck Three, Stefan was addressing the entire exploration team. Though the pontoon was winched up and the doors firmly closed, the cold of the channel still seeped through like an alien spirit. Feet were stamping.

'So we'll be talking to those we haven't already spoken to about Ralph. Try to remember where and when you last saw him. Times would be good. In the meantime, definitely do not mention anything about this to our guests. OK? Now, back to your duties, please.' As they gratefully began to disperse, he added: 'Not you, Heidi.'

Beckoning her to follow, he led her down a side corridor to a quiet corner out of the cold, with just two seats.

'*Mach dir keine Sorgen,*' he said, holding his hands up. He continued in German. 'I'm not accusing you of anything. We all know about your disagreement with some of Ralph's opinions. The incident with the French TV people was unfortunate...'

'Incident?' said Heidi. 'I just answered questions, as we were asked to.'

'Whatever. My point is it's history. His disappearance is more important. Until he turns up, smiling and healthy...'

'When did he ever smile?'

Stefan took a deep breath.

'Until then, Nils and his team will be investigating everything and he's bound to ask you two key questions, so I'm asking you first to help you think about your answers. OK?'

'OK.'

'First, was... is your disagreement with Ralph anything personal? Have you had private arguments? Are you in fact enemies?'

'No. I just avoid him when I can. I'm not the only one who thinks he's creepy. I wouldn't have anything in private with him, arguments or otherwise.' She shuddered at the thought.

It wasn't quite the answer Stefan expected, but he made no comment.

'And,' he continued, 'when did you last see him?'

Heidi thought for a moment.

'On the landing yesterday. I was on duty by one of the cones where there was a drop down to the glacier. I saw Ralph go past uphill.'

'Was he alone?'

'Yes. He had some equipment though. Weather monitoring, I suppose.'

'Did you see him come back?'

'No. Soon after, I handed over to Jimmy.'

'OK.'

'But he came back aboard anyway, didn't he?'

'Yes. He seems to have gone AWOL after that. OK, thanks.'

Just as Heidi was walking off, she turned to face her boss again.

'Stefan,' she said, 'this is turning into the worst voyage I've been on down here. I didn't think I'd ever say this, but I'm glad it's the last of the season.'

*

A few hours later, the mood was more positive among the passengers in the bar. After being dispersed on their various activities the previous day, the Usual Suspects (they'd begun to think of themselves as an official grouping) were assembling for an aperatif before dinner – including Danielle, who'd felt unwell, only emerging from her cabin to keep Maisie company while she sketched.

'Fit again, Dani?' asked Lennox.

'Aye. Must have caught Fi's bug. Hey, you didn't tell us your wife's so talented. Have you brought any of your sketches to show, Maisie?'

'Oh, no one'd be interested in those. Look, what's this?'

On their table – in fact on every table – another 'MISSING' poster had been placed.

'Oh no,' said Fiona, 'not another man overboard.'

Vernon read it out:

Dr Ralph Dulacki, American, 46 (above), a member of our Expedition Team, has not been seen since 15:15 yesterday 27th February, when he returned aboard from the landing in Andvord Bay. I am very concerned for his safety. If anyone has seen Dr Dulacki since then (please check your photos and videos) or has any relevant information, please report to me or to any member of the crew at once. Capt U Thommessen

'Well,' said Lennox, 'it's the climate guy. So that's why this morning's lecture was cancelled. I was looking forward to that. Hey, honey, maybe you drew Dr D in one of your pictures. He's pretty obvious with his glasses and that superior look. You'd better check 'em out.'

While Maisie went back to her cabin, the others began swiping through the photos on their phones. Except Harry.

'Not got your phone, Harry?' asked Lennox.

'Nor camera,' he said. 'I still think it's weird people associate photographs with a telephone. No, I prefer to just remember what I've seen. After all, it's pretty unforgettable round here.'

'Gee, you're a one-off, you know that? I been sending shots back to my kids every day, even videos.'

'Well, there's no family to see mine. And my friends have been everywhere, seen everything. Even here, some of them.'

Fiona chipped in.

'Family, that's what you need, Harry. It's what we've been put on this Earth for, when all's said and done.'

'By whom?' Wary of the oft-repeated advice from his friends back home not to get involved in religious arguments, Harry had been carefully steering clear of the subject with the obviously Catholic Fiona. Somehow, after a gulp or two of beer, his guard was down.

'By the Lord, of course.'

'So not only do you believe in this supernatural being, but you think you know his objectives as well?'

By now the others were listening. Danielle had even settled back in her chair, nursing her wine. Vernon was unusually quiet.

'We're all here to be tested, to repent our sins and serve the Lord.'

'And if you have no sins?'

'We're all sinful. Especially you, Harry, in your godless world. I'll be praying for you.'

Harry laughed. He heard the sneer in his voice and half of him didn't much like the sound of it.

'Save your prayers for those missing at sea, Fiona. Not that they'll make any difference. And anyway, there's no such thing as sin – it's just a Christian invention. The rest of us call it right and wrong.'

'Taking the Lord's name in vain is surely wrong.'

'When did I do that?'

'You called him supernatural.'

He laughed again, a contemptuous laugh.

'And the Lord's name is? Just so I'm on the alert.'

'God, the Lord Almighty.'

By now Fiona was no longer looking at Harry but down at her wine, almost praying. He considered dropping the subject, but just couldn't resist ploughing on while he was on form.

'What's natural is all around us. You can't miss it, Fiona. But nowhere in nature, so far as I'm aware – and I've watched all the David Attenboroughs – is there anything – animal, vegetable or mineral – with the ability to place a new, fully-fledged, reproducing species on a distant planet. That's what I'd call a *super* ability. Supernatural is precisely the word for your God.'

Fiona stood up, a little shakily, handbag over her shoulder.

'I don't have to stay here,' she said, 'and listen to this... this blasphemy!'

As she walked off, Harry took a long draught of his beer. It was Lennox who broke the awkward silence.

'You may have gone too far there, my friend.'

'She had it coming,' said Danielle, to everyone's surprise, including Harry, unaware he had an ally. 'But maybe we'd better stay apart for dinner tonight.'

'Don't worry,' said Harry. 'You can tell Fiona she's safe. I've already got a dinner date.

*

At the back of the restaurant was a double swing door leading to a separate room. Beside it stood a steward in a mauve jacket, rather than the white of other restaurant and bar staff. It was here that Harry had been invited to present himself for dinner with Nils Bakke and Captain Thommessen, a meeting he hoped would confirm Clemente's progress to a safe harbour in Chile. The dining room comprised just six tables, all with a view over the stern, beyond which the *Sturlanga*'s wake formed the only recognisable shape in a quickly darkening seascape. Harry was shown to the farthest table, laid for two.

'Are you sure this is the right one?' Harry asked the mauve steward. 'I think there are three of us.'

'The Captain ordered for just two places, sir. Can I get you a drink?'

As the steward walked away, he bowed very slightly to the advancing Captain Thommessen, resplendent in freshly pressed white shirt and blue epaulettes.

'Harry,' she said, holding out her hand. 'I'm glad you could join me.'

'No Security Officer, Captain?' he said, standing.

'Nils is busy. And please call me Ulrika.'

Perhaps it was a date after all, he thought. Interesting.

With drinks and menu choices sorted and a few pleasantries exchanged, Harry raised the topic he'd expected to talk about.

'Is Clemente safely in Chile, Ulrika?'

'No, no. It takes two days across the Drake and PA – Punta Arenas – is way beyond that anyway. The *Grettis* is due there the day after tomorrow, but I'll let you know the latest before you disembark in Ushuaia if you want.'

'Yes, please, if you have time.'

'It's the least we can do. I don't mind telling you I was relieved to resolve that issue at least. Without you, he might not have come forward at all – and who knows what would have happened?'

'But it's not really resolved, is it? The gunman's still on board...' She gestured him to lower his voice. '... still on board somewhere, maybe still looking for our friend.'

'In a sense I hope he is still looking, rather than guessing he's on his way to Chile. By the way, yes, we've identified Argentinian passengers and crew – or those with known Argentinian connections – and done extra checks. Nothing obvious.'

They leant back as the first course arrived: mozzarella with roasted red peppers.

'I meant to ask,' resumed Harry, 'Whose territory are we in here? In the politics lecture they said Argentina and the UK both claim this section of Antarctica.'

'They do and the Antarctic Treaty acknowledges both claims and, as with all other national claims, effectively ignores them. *Bon appetit.*'

'Mmm,' mumbled Harry, mouth half-full, before pursuing the point when he could. 'I mean who do you report crimes to?'

'There's not a single answer, Harry. This a Norwegian-registered vessel and so obviously I report all incidents, including the other night's, back to HQ in Oslo. We can also charge people for offences under Norwegian law, but if a suspect is found for an offence on Antarctic soil – not that that's likely – they can be charged in their home country. There's no Antarctic-wide law enforcement – it's more of a pity. Is that the right phrase?'

'More's the pity. Although that doesn't make grammatical sense.'

'A lot of things round here don't make sense.'

Harry thought this might be the Captain's way into whatever had prompted the invitation, but the main course (medallions of beef fillet *alla Romana*) was accompanied just by a light-hearted discussion on the oddities of English. Entertaining as this was, by the time walnut tart and coffee arrived, Harry was beginning to think that's all there was to it, but his hostess suddenly turned to face him.

'Harry,' she said. 'You're very patient. You must be wondering why I invited you to a dinner for two.' So it *was* planned, thought Harry. He shrugged. 'To be honest, I simply needed a break from my duties. Right now I feel like a scientist reading genome sequences.' She waited till he raised his eyebrows. 'Just one thing after another.'

Harry laughed.

'Maybe you should try stand-up comedy instead,' he said.

'Hm, I know where my skills are and it's not there. The thing is, this latest problem – you've seen my notice about Dr Dulacki?' He nodded. As she'd avoided the subject, so had he. 'I don't think my skills or any of my team's skills are up to solving mysteries – detective work is what it is.' She looked Harry straight in the eye for a few seconds.

'Er, nor mine,' he said, taking a sip of coffee. 'I'm a semi-retired property consultant, not a detective. And this time I'm not a witness to anything to do with Dr Dulacki either... so far as I'm aware.'

'It'd be beyond coincidence if you were, Harry. No, I just wondered if I might run what I know past you – is that the phrase?' He nodded. Her English really was better than most native speakers. 'To see if anything occurs to you, as an outsider. To be honest, we're at a bit of a loss and another point of view can do no harm.'

'Well, Ulrika, as our American friends say: shoot!'

With wine on top of beer, his own English was becoming a little too relaxed. The Captain, of course, drank water.

'OK.' she began. 'here's what we have.'

As she ran through the basic facts of Ralph Dulacki's disappearance, Harry briefly considered making notes on his napkin but, aware of the pretension, in the end he trusted to memory. After she concluded with Stefan's finding that none of the Zodiac pilots remembered taxi-ing Ralph back to the *Sturlanga*, he played for time by ordering another coffee – after all, back here with the posh set it was actually drinkable. Central American. Guatemala? Eventually, he attempted a summary.

'Right,' he said, hoping he sounded decisive. 'You think Ralph came back aboard safely, don't you?'

She nodded.

'The computer says he did and his coat and boots are in his cabin. With just cabin card and phone missing, I think he left his cabin sometime yesterday afternoon or evening and never went back.'

'And he doesn't secretly drink?'

'Very unlikely.'

There was a sensitive elephant in the dining room and Harry needed to expose it.

'You haven't told me whether there's any reason he might have taken his own life.'

'That's because no one knows any. I've been in touch with his colleagues at Rothera Station, 400k south of here, to find out if anyone's heard from him recently. They're asking round, but the station chief says Ralph keeps his research work there and his job with us separate. No close friends there, he thinks. I'm holding off contacting his family in the US till I absolutely have to.'

'Hm. His cabin card may have come back aboard without him, of course.'

'You've seen our process. Two beeps instead of one would be pretty obvious.'

'It could have been just one.'

'But then the person who brought it back would be registered as missing.'

'And were they? We've all heard calls for passengers to report to Reception. I guess some of these are names the computer thinks never returned from a landing, but when they show up at Reception alive and well, the computer's updated manually.'

'That's exactly what happens, Harry. Your guesses are right.'

'So was there any manual update after that landing?'

Once again the Captain stared straight at Harry. He thought he detected the slightest flicker of panic in them.

'I'll find out,' she said. And Captain Thommessen did make a note on her napkin.

'And then there's the equipment?'

'What equipment?'

'You said he was seen taking some equipment ashore. Is it back in his cabin – or wherever it belongs?'

Another note.

'Very good,' she said. 'Anything else?'

Once again there was something nagging at the back of his mind, reluctant to come to the front.

'No, Ulrika, but if I think of anything else...'

'Ask for me at Reception.'

'Or Nils?'

'Preferably me.'

What may be going on between Captain and Security Officer Harry had no idea. They stood up. Thanking him profusely for his help, the Captain nodded to the steward and was already heading back into the main restaurant when Harry called her back.

'Yes, Harry?' she said, coming back and standing close enough for them to keep their voices low.

'You could check the size of those boots too.'

*

It was the *Sturlanga*'s radio officer who phoned Captain Thommessen with the message the next morning. Despite a late night and her growing list of unresolved issues, she'd slept soundly and after the early rounds had just got back to her cabin for a coffee.

'It's Pedersen, Captain.'

'Yes, Kristoffer.'

'Gonzalo Videla has distributed a photograph of a body they found just after dawn.' She immediately knew what was coming. 'Captain, it's Ralph Dulacki.'

PART

THREE

CRISIS

Murder in Antarctica

17

After lunch

The throb of the helicopter's motor had soon drowned out the background hum of the *Sturlanga*'s engine. Its shaky landing in the gusts of wind around Deck Nine's helipad had been witnessed at a distance by the knot of frustrated passengers hoping to take their post-prandial stroll, but once again barred from the open deck by locked doors. These included Harry, accompanied by the usual crowd. Speculation on the chopper's business was rife. Lennox suggested a doctor to attend a seriously ill passenger, Vernon imagined a detective from Scotland Yard to investigate the disappearance of Dr Dulacki, while Fiona combined both in response to what she suggested might to be the discovery of a body in the ship's engine room. Quite why there, she didn't reveal. Surely, they all agreed, there would be an explanatory announcement soon.

They were right about the announcement. Wrong about its content.

It came a whole hour after the helicopter had touched down and a short man in winter gear and ski boots had been seen walking across the deck, escorted by a crew member. It was the captain's clear tones that immediately silenced every other sound in all public areas.

'Ladies and Gentlemen, your attention please. This is Captain

Thommessen. We have now left the Antarctic Peninsula and are on a northerly course which will pass by the south-westerly tip of the South Shetland Islands and continue directly into Drake Passage. There will be no further landings. We expect to arrive in Ushuaia ahead of schedule late tomorrow night. In the meantime a serious situation has arisen. You are all instructed to return to your cabins within the next hour and remain there until further notice. Dinner will be served in your cabins. I repeat: please return to your cabins by sixteen hundred hours – four o'clock – and remain there until advised otherwise. There will be no further announcements for the moment.'

As passengers throughout the vessel stared at each other in disbelief, there followed the same message in French, German and Spanish, spoken by other members of the crew.

*

At four fifteen exactly a firm knock sounded on Harry's cabin door.

'You are to come with me, please, Mr Pound,' said the young woman he recognised as Nils' colleague, the Assistant Security Officer. He now also realised she was the Filipina who'd relieved him of his passport at embarkation, a short but sturdy woman who was clearly no stranger to strenuous exercise. Her name badge read Angel Bautista. Right now she looked anything but angelic.

'Where are we going?' asked Harry, as he pulled on his shoes.

'Immediately,' said the stone-faced Angel.

Having taken the lift in silence, they emerged on Deck Eight, where Harry was led through a deserted bar to the Expedition Library. Or what had previously been the Expedition Library. All the books and maps had been removed, to be replaced by just a pair of laptop computers on the map table. In front of one sat Nils, in front of the other a small man: fifties, dishevelled grey hair, thick glasses. As Harry approached he didn't raise his eyes from the screen.

Standing to greet Harry was Captain Thommessen. No hand was offered.

'Mr Pound,' she said, this is Politioverbetjent Harket of the Norwegian Police. Detective Inspector in English. Please answer his questions – and do as he says. I shall leave you to it.' Gone was the genial and expansive dinner companion of the previous evening. In her place a tired and grey-faced woman. 'We followed up your ideas about the cabin cards – and you were right about the boots too.'

With this, she walked away.

The man named Harket said something in Norwegian to Nils, who promptly followed his Captain. Left alone with the bespectacled policeman, Harry was unsure whether to remain standing, but did so in silence. After a minute, Harket looked up from the screen and gesticulated to the seat vacated by Nils. Harry sat down. Still no words. Carefully closing the laptop, Harket picked up a notebook and pen, swivelled his seat towards Harry and removed his heavy reading glasses. The Nordic eyes that looked directly at the English passenger were startlingly blue and yet devoid of any decipherable expression – except perhaps intense concentration.

'We have little time,' he began, 'and so I will arrive immediately at the point. Forty-eight hours ago I was at my office in the Royal Norwegian Embassy in Buenos Aires. Now, after three flights and one uncomfortable night at an air base on King George Island, I find myself on board a cruise ship with over six hundred passengers and crew. I was told there had been a serious incident aboard, an attempted murder. The perpetrated must still be on board...'

'Perpetrator.' Harry's interruption prompted five seconds of silence.

'... and is probably still armed. It is my instruction to identify him or her before docking at Ushuaia. On arrival I find that a second suspicious death has occurred.' Harry's raised eyebrows prompted a raised hand. 'I shall explain in a moment. One possible murder, one attempted murder. And...' He glanced at his notebook. '... approximately 623 suspects. You are among them, Mr Pound.'

'What? I don't even...' started Harry, but was once again silenced by the raised hand. His undisguised sigh signalled, at least to himself, that he'd decided to let Inspector Harket finish. Whenever that would be. As he spoke, there was something about the policeman that demanded – and expected – an utter focus from whomever was in his company.

'But you're not here as a suspect. You're here as an assistant. I should say as a willing assistant, I hope.' The last two words escaped as if a reluctantly revealed chink in a warrior's armour. 'I am aware that you are involved not only in the attempt on the life of Señor Gil but also in the disappearance of Mr Challinor. I am not yet aware of any involvement of yours in the death of Dr Dulacki – although my mind is opened. However, my time at the air base was useful. With the help of both Captain Thommessen and...' Another glance at the notebook. '... the Devon County Police in England I am convinced not only of your probable innocence but also of your remarkable skills of analysis and deduction in the sort of investigation I must make. *We* must make. While I am not precisely happy to ask for the assistance of a suspect, I have no choice. My English is – as you have no doubt observed – not perfect. We have potentially hundreds of people to interview, many English-speaking. I find some English accents... undeciphered.'

'Indecipherable,' ventured Harry.

'Indeed. You understand the Americans too?'

'In their speech, yes.'

The implication was lost on Harket.

'Then I ask you to help me solve two mysteries in less than two days.'

The silence filled the space around them.

'I'm very sorry to hear of Dr Dulacki's death. Of course I will help you,' said Harry. 'But only two mysteries? Aren't there three?'

'Mr Challinor? A man overboard is not so uncommon as you might think. It's a clean type of suicide. With no suspicious circumstances, so far as I know, I think we can leave that one, don't you?'

'If you say so...' Harry just stopped himself adding 'sir'.

'You will address me as Inspector Harket. I will address you as Mr Pound. Any questions before I summarize our... our *modus operandi*, Mr Pound?'

Of the many that flitted through Harry's churning mind, he chose just one. For the moment.

'Yes, Inspector. This is a police matter, a security matter. Why ask *me* to help, a mere passenger, when there are more qualified people among the crew?'

'A fair question. There are two answers. One: because no one is above suspicion and my guess – I think you say *educated* guess – is that you will be more impartial in our investigations than others. Two – and I would be pleased if you mention this to no one?' Harry nodded. 'In my view, the manner in which the responsible crew of *MS Sturlanga* have dealt with these incidents so far is not sufficiently professional and does not give sufficient priority to the safety of hundreds of members of the public. This is why I committed you all to your cabins.'

'Confined us,' ventured Harry.

'By the way, you will not now return to your own cabin unless absolutely necessary. Agreed?' Despite idly wondering about practicalities – food and sleep came to mind – Harry felt that disagreeing with Harket might be complicated. He nodded. 'Very well. This is how we shall proceed...'

*

One hundred and sixty miles due south of the *Sturlanga* a delicate operation was taking place, not helped by sub-zero temperatures and a strengthening wind. Having completed his initial examination of the body he now knew to be that of Dr Ralph Dulacki, the Chilean Medical Officer at González Videla had finally given the go-ahead to move the semi-frozen corpse from the snow-covered ledge where the morning shift had spotted it. After several years in which Dulacki had effectively made the Antarctic mainland his home, his final departure from it was an awkward one. Before lifting the body into the inflatable, the two young naval officers wrapped the body in the strongest sheet they'd been able to lay their hands on in the base at short notice. The fact that a Chilean national flag was being used to transport an American citizen didn't seem inappropriate to them at all: among most living here on the frozen continent, all nationalities were as one, all sufferings as one and all priorities as one. It's the tourists that bring the trouble, they thought. And so it was with a strange sense of restoring their own priorities that, once back at the base's small landing stage and up the penguin-lined path to the small cluster of shacks that formed their temporary home, they gently placed the body on a table. The same table had only recently been cleared of trinkets for sale to cruise passengers. They unwrapped their cargo. If any reminder were needed that they were living in a hostile environment, this was it. All exposed parts of Dulacki's skin were coloured blue, grey or black. Respectful of both the deceased and the task ahead for the Medical Officer, they withdrew in silence.

18

Dinnertime

The rattling of trolleys and a mix of spicy aromas drifted from the stairwell across the empty bar to the Expedition Library where Inspector Harket and Nils Bakke sat at a table whose laptops had now been joined by a spread of files, papers and photographs. Angel Bautista was putting the finishing touches to an incident board where the map wall used to be. Just one large-scale map entitled 'Graham Land' and showing the tip if the Antarctic Peninsula, had been retained. Harry himself was seated some way away at one of the bar tables, where he'd been given the job of perusing full-length photos of the ship's maritime crew, expedition crew and hospitality staff, with the specific task of setting aside those who definitely could *not* have been the figure who shot at Clemente Gil on the open deck. If the signs of the dinner they were missing affected any of the four, they didn't show it.

Harket signalled to Harry to follow him to the other side of the bar, where they stood looking out of a port-side window over the rolling and ever-darkening swell that separated this small, mobile outpost of civilisation from a four-thousand-metre drop to the seabed below. The Norwegian turned to the much taller Englishman. He was obliged to crane his neck upwards as he spoke.

'Mr Pound, you haven't asked how Ralph Dulacki died,' he said.

'I assumed you'd tell me when you were ready.'

Harket nodded.

'In a sense it's a remarkable tale, but I'll give you the bare bones. Ah, perhaps not the best phrase.' Away from the inspector's makeshift desk in the makeshift office, Harry sensed a slight change in his manner. Harket held up an A4 sheet showing an enlargement from the wall map. 'Dr Dulacki was last seen alive about noon the day before yesterday right here, where the A is marked, a little away from the landing site in Andvord Bay. He was carrying meteorological equipment uphill across the snow to here, where the B is marked. We know it was here because a party from the nearby Chilean naval base has a few hours ago made a landing, found the equipment still there and sent photographs. Dulacki's body was found just after dawn this morning where C is marked.'

'Good grief!' exclaimed Harry.

'Indeed. It's about five kilometres away, seven the way we think he walked.'

'How do you know, Inspector?'

'Boot prints. Even though it snowed there over the last forty-eight hours, they say it's clear in which direction he left B and arrived at C. He knew the geography around there, knew the nearest settlement and knew the only sure route was round the coastline.'

Harket paused. With a host of questions occurring to Harry, he wondered if the pause was to allow room for him to ask them. A sort of test. He started with the obvious one.

'So he nearly made it?'

'Yes.'

'Remarkable, as you say. Did they find a phone on him or even a compass?'

'We're waiting to hear. There's a medical officer at the base dealing with the body.'

Harry nodded and slowly stroked his chin until he realised it might look a little pretentious.

'Back at Andvord Bay, were there any other footprints between A and B?'

'Important question. We have the description from the Chileans and photographs. They're not police officers and weren't as careful as they could be. But, yes, it seems there is much more disturbing in the snow between A and B than between B and C.'

'Someone was with him. Any sign of a struggle?'

'Nothing away from the equipment.'

Another pause. As the two men looked out from their safe, warm lounge to the hostile environment that lay just beyond the glass, Harry's thoughts strayed to the horror of being trapped alone in the cold and dark, with your little floating module of security having disappeared. Harket's voice brought him back to the here and now.

'What do you think happened out there, Mr Pound?'

Harry turned to Harket.

'It was obviously no suicide. The ship would know you were missing and look for you – and anyway, why walk towards safety rather than away from it?'

Harket nodded. Harry continued.

'It could have been an accident: he dozed off and the ship was gone. Except that – correct me if I'm wrong – his cabin card was returned and the boots in his cabin were not his?'

'Wrong size. The ideas you gave the Captain were good. The staff delivering dinner to the cabins have been told to look at the boots lent to each passenger and report any missing. On the passengers who had to be found as their cabin cards had not been registered, we have a list and will interview them soon. It seems certain there was a foul.'

'Foul play,' said Harry after a moment. 'Yes, someone has

followed Dulacki up the hill – or went up *with* him?'

'A witness says he walked up alone.'

'Someone has followed him, disabled him in some way, taken his cabin card and left him there. To die, presumably.'

'My conclusion also.'

'So we know the how. What we don't know is the who... and...'

'And the why,' completed Harket. 'One will lead us to the other. Now, Mr Pound, do you have anything else you'd like to share with me? Any odd behaviour on board, any – I think you call them oddities – any relevant oddities at all?'

Vernon's interchangeable accents, thought Harry, were certainly odd, but surely not in the 'relevant' category.

'No, Inspector' he said. 'Nothing.'

*

As Harry and Harket were walking back to the library, a passenger two decks below found his dinner interrupted by a loud knock on the cabin door. Three minutes later he was being escorted into a meeting room where Captain Thommessen stood with her back to the door. As it closed, she turned.

'Monsieur Girault,' she began. 'Are you behind the reports of a scientist missing in Antarctica that are appearing in the news media?'

Benoit held his hands out wide.

'Captain, we are imprisoned in our cabins. I'm sure most of the passengers have been emailing and texting.'

'Was one of them you?'

'I have filed reports of course.'

'Of course? Of course?! What did I tell you?'

The blue eyes stood out from her pale face like jewels in a crown of linen.

'Of course I have to do my job.'

'Among those who read the news was Dr Dulacki's wife. Do you want to know how I know?' He didn't answer. ' I know because I've just finished a phone call with her. A difficult and upsetting conversation, as you can imagine. Or perhaps you can't. Are you even capable of imagining anything beyond yourself and your so-called job, Monsieur Girault?'

He looked down at his expensive Parisian deck shoes.

'You will come with me to meet someone,' she said.

*

After hearing Captain Thommessen's brief account, Inspector Harket dismissed the Frenchman with a crew member as chaperone, instructed to keep him away from his cabin for fifteen minutes. He then turned to the Captain.

'In those fifteen minutes, Captain, you will disable all the passengers' wi-fi. Why you didn't do this before is a matter for a later discussion.'

'But...'

Whatever her buts were no one would hear, since Harket had already turned away and towards the incident board. She left the library promptly.

With the four of them – Harket, Bakke, Bautista and Harry – facing the incident board, with its neatly placed maps, photographs and felt-tipped notes, a whole minute passed before Harket spoke.

'What do we see? We see two incidents: the shooting at Gil Clemente and the death of Ralph Dulacki. The shooting is the most urgent to solve because the shooter and the weapon are probably still aboard and therefore a danger to everyone. The death... no, wait. Bautista, please change that title to "*Murder* of Ralph Dulacki". There seems little doubt now.' As she did so, he continued. 'We have no reason to believe Dr Dulacki's murderer is armed or planning another action. So, although more important, I assess it as less urgent... unless... yes, now that Bautista has correctly drawn a dotted line between the two, to represent an unknown, we must ask ourselves: could there be a connection between these two incidents?'

The pause was long enough to suggest his question was not rhetorical. Harry briefly considered raising once again the matter of the third incident, the disappearance of Joseph Challinor, but decided to keep quiet. Instead, it was Nils Bakke who spoke.

'There could be a very direct connection, Inspector. The shooter and the killer could be the same person.'

'Aha!' Harket raised his right forefinger as he spoke. 'Very good. Could they indeed? Why could one man – or one woman – want to kill both an undercover Spanish police officer and a respected American climate scientist? Ideas?'

'Dr Dulacki was also involved in the drug trade?' suggested Bakke.

'Put it on a list, Bautista.'

Her flip-chart had been at the ready. Inside, Angel Bautista was swelling with pride at her involvement in what amounted to detective work. From stewardess to admin to security, her career path seemed suddenly to have embarked on an upward trend.

'Both had witnessed something here on board?' she said, with some hesitation.

'Quite possible. On the other hand, maybe the shooting was a case of mistaken identity. In the dark the shooter thought Gil was Dulacki. Put them both on. Mr Pound?'

'Clemente and Dr Dulacki are quite different body shapes. Going through those crew photos has helped me focus on what I saw on deck that night. I've rejected those who couldn't possibly have been the person who shot at Clemente and I'm left with just nine people of the right stature.'

'Good. Please bring them over. We're not ruling out passengers of course, but with the check shirt as the only other clue, we've got to narrow it down somehow.'

Harry and Bautista pinned the nine photographs on the board.

'As you can see, with one exception they're all men,' said Harry.

They all stared at the exception.

'Captain Thommessen?', whispered Bakke, looking around. 'Surely... I mean...'

'I'm implying nothing,' stressed Harry. 'Just going by physique.'

'Should I take that one down, Inspector?' asked Bautista.

He thought for a moment. The slightest trace of a smile could be detected behind the thick glasses.'

'No,' he said. 'Leave it there.'

All four studied the line of photographs for a while, until Harry spoke, more to himself than the others.

'I think I know who it is.'

They all turned to him.

'Go ahead, Mr Pound,' said Harket.

'Why would someone go outside on a cold Antarctic night in a short-sleeved shirt? Because they'd just taken off something more visible: a white jacket, for instance. Who could leave the bar on Deck Nine without being seen by the barman? Well, the barman himself of course.'

He tapped on the image of a tall, muscular young man with a neat beard, jet-black hair pulled back into a pony tail. Harket and Bautista stared at it. Bakke looked at the floor. Harket approached the board to read the name, but Bakke spoke first.

'It's Luís Moreno,' he said quietly. 'Argentinian, twenty-six.'

'Your memory is impressive, Officer Bakke,' said Harket. 'Do you know his cabin number too?'

'He won't be in his cabin, Inspector. In fact he's not on board at all.'

As they all turned to him, Bakke raised his head.

'Moreno's on the *Grettis*. He left at the same time as Clemente Gil.'

19

After putting in an immediate call to the Captain to contact the *Grettis*, Nils Bakke explained. All four were now standing in front of the incident board.

'Moreno was taken ill, quite suddenly I remember. Dr Schneider – the Medical Officer – recognised the symptoms as likely to indicate an infectious virus, one of the Sars group, and took the opportunity of the Zodiac going over to the *Grettis* to get him back to port as soon as possible.' The image of a third person in the Zodiac with Clemente immediately came to Harry's mind. 'But the test done by the *Grettis*'s MO came back negative, so we took no further action. By then the *Grettis* was away of course.'

Harket looked at Security Officer.

'And when we were going through the numbers on board, Bakke,' he said, 'you didn't think to mention they are not three down – Challinor, Gil and Dulacki – than the numbers at embarkation, but *four* down?' The inspector emphasised the new number with the fingers of his right hand.

'Well, I...'

'Never mind. We have more urgent matters.' He straightened his short stature to its full height. 'Now, is there any doubt that Moreno is our man?'

It was Bautista who spoke first.

'The check shirt,' she said. 'It doesn't fit in. Only the expedition crew wears them. The bar staff have dark shirts under their jackets.'

Harry had been mulling over the same point.

'Before I went out on deck I didn't look at him, but when I went back, I sat for a while at the bar and – I'm pretty sure – he was dressed as normal. I'd been there a few times. Maybe he kept a different shirt for just such an occasion, to disguise himself a little.'

'Does it matter?' asked Bakke, eager to recover some lost credibility. 'Everything else adds up. We must get a warning to Gil – unless we're already too late.'

'Proof,' said Harry simply. 'The inspector asks if there's any doubt. I don't remember seeing much luggage in the Zodiac, if any at all. Did Moreno leave his belongings here?'

'Yes,' said Bakke. 'With the chance of infection, we immediately packed up all his stuff. It's in a bag in the Medical Centre.'

'We must speak with Dr Schneider anyway,' said Harket. 'Bakke, come with me. You two stay here.'

Bautista threw a pleading look to Harry. He knew what was behind it.

'Inspector Harket,' he said. 'May we get something to eat?'

'Oh yes, go ahead.'

'And, er...' started Bakke. But the inspector was already on his way out.

'With me, Bakke.' he said.

*

Benoit Girault wasn't the only passenger disgruntled at losing wi-fi. Within seconds of the brief announcement, which gave neither explanation nor timescale, heads were popping out of cabin doors, some of them still in the process of consuming their meal.

'Would anyone care to tell me what's going on?' asked Fiona Phelan on Deck Six.

'I don't know myself, madam,' said a passing steward, 'but would you please stay inside your cabin? It's our orders.'

'Ha! Just obeying orders. Now where have I heard that before, Danielle?'

But her friend didn't answer. With the Drake beginning to shake, she lay half-asleep under the duvet.

Two decks down, Lennox Montgomery, until now happy to follow instructions – at least happier than Maisie – had had enough and stood in the corridor exchanging gestures of exasperation with fellow passengers, before walking a few yards along to Harry's cabin and rapping on the door.

'Harry!' he called. 'Help us out here. You usually know what the hell's goin' on. You must be in there.'

*

But Harry was four decks above in the main bar, tucking into a plate stacked with salmon pasta in the pleasant company of Angel Bautista. Only now did he notice the rolling of the *Sturlanga*. Concentrating on the investigation, under the intense supervision of Inspector Harket, must have taken all his attention. As the young Security Officer recounted tales of the rough seas of her childhood in the Philippines, he also realised Louise Kennet had been absent from his thoughts for the longest time since the news had arrived from England. Wondering if Sami had uncovered any more information on that score, he felt for his phone – before realising he too would now be subject to the communications blackout.

Harry and Angel were just discussing how long this might last when Harket burst into the bar.

'It's him all right,' he said, not looking at the room's only other occupants and striding straight to the library. 'It's Luís Moreno.'

Immediately leaving their unfinished meal, they followed him. He was already at the board scrawling on blank sheets with a black felt tip.

'Proof indeed, Mr Pound,' he said without looking round. 'Yet again your hunch was right. Do you say hunch?' He didn't wait for a reply. 'Not only a check shirt identical to the expedition crew's, but also in his bag a gun! *The* gun, I'm sure. Forced to make quick decisions to follow his prey onto the *Grettis*, he dumped his weapon. It'd be scanned on boarding the other ship. He should have dropped it over the side of the dinghy.' A pause. 'Our man is panicking. He makes mistakes. This means two things: opportunity and danger.'

'What about Clemente, Inspector?' asked Harry. 'Has anyone heard from the *Grettis*? Is he all right?'

'So far. Maybe.' Roughly pulling Moreno's photo off the board, he turned to Bautista. 'Clear this half away, please.'

With that, the Norwegian whirlwind slumped into his seat, looked back at the board and let out a sigh. Harry sat down beside him. He considered asking after Nils Bakke, but sensed they ought to wait for the Inspector's update.

'Three points,' said Harket suddenly, holding up three fingers. 'One, the *MS Grettis* docked early in Punta Arenas. Moreno was kept in isolation by the MO all the time, despite his negative test, and so Gil arrived safely. Knowing a fellow police officer was in potential danger from any local contacts of Grupo 21, the PA police picked him up immediately and took him to safety. Two – and this is the bad news – Moreno has also disembarked. Our message arrived just too late. An alert has been put out of course, but my guess is he's disappeared into town and could be anywhere. We've lost him.'

For a moment he stared at the empty table in front of him.

'You said three, sir,' said Bautista.

'Ah yes. And three – good news that follows from two. As far as we're concerned, we're off that case. We've identified the perpe... perpetrator and given the Chilean police almost all we know. Bakke is right now sending them background information on Moreno. And now it's up to them.'

'But he's not caught,' said Harry. 'Surely that's not good news.'

'It is for us. It means we can concentrate on the Dulacki case.' Harket waved a hand at the half of the board that remained full. 'And it's especially good news for you, Mr Pound...' Harry turned to face him. '... Because you're free to return to your cabin. I'm afraid to say I've not been entirely honest with you. You were absolutely right: it would indeed be odd if I asked a member of the public to act as a detective – even a member as smart as you. The reason I wanted you here is nothing to do with understanding strange English. It's that, as long as an enemy of Clemente Gil was aboard – an armed enemy – you were his most likely target. It was you who spent time with Gil, listened to his story. If he had information to pass on about Grupo 21, information too important to trust to the internet, it's you he would have told. I wanted you where I could see you all the time.'

'Well, you did that. But Gil didn't tell me anything important anyway.'

'But the gunman – Moreno – didn't know that. No, Bakke, Bautista and I will manage from here. Please get some sleep.' At this, Angel Bautista shrugged. Her own bed had been calling for a while. 'Of course, when you wake up, if you have any bright ideas about the Dulacki case, please feel free to come up here again. We'll still be here.'

With a brief nod and a passing thought for Baustista's and Bakke's missing sleep, Harry made a quick exit. His cabin now seemed a precious haven.

20

Early the next morning

Behind the jagged black peaks that surrounded Ushuaia, the dawn pushed streaks of dark blue into the skies above Tierra de Fuego. On the rippling surface of the Beagle Strait the night lights of the city spread parallel reflections towards the jetty, where, a day ahead of schedule, the *MS Sturlanga* had recently docked. From her upper decks it would have been a bewitching scene for the vessel's return to the cold lights of civilisation, even if this was still 'the end of the world'. Nut no-one had been outside to enjoy it.

Inside, however, there was plenty of activity. For most of the passengers it was the first time since teenage years that they'd been confined to their rooms. And for many it was the first for a long time that they'd been denied access to both the internet and a phone signal. A sense of mutiny was in the air. Heads were out of cabin doors, indignation rumbled down the corridors, mild abuse was directed at any crew member in sight. As for the latter, many were exhausted after a long, late shift serving food and drink to the cabins – for little thanks. Senior officers had already been awake for some time, going back and forth from meeting to phone to internet (their connection still being open) in an attempt to adjust schedules, cancel arrangements, tentatively make new ones and even investigate the insurance implications that would surely follow such a disrupted voyage.

Among the few still sleeping soundly were Harket and his temporary team of two. At about one o'clock, the inspector had finally seen sense, closed down the incident room and given Bakke and Bautista permission to sleep as long as they wanted – or until he had them woken. And reluctantly, after beginning to lose concentration, he'd granted himself five hours sleep. Captain Thommessen had allocated him her own guest cabin, the one recently occupied by Clemente Gil, as well as the services of her own steward Maria. Harket's requirements, however, were simple: a strong coffee at six o'clock, with no disturbance before that unless something urgent cropped up. By the time coffee was delivered, two people were waiting along the corridor for his attention, one rather more impatiently than the other. Maria showed Captain Thommessen in.

'Good morning, Captain,' said Harket, fully dressed and perched on the edge of the bed. 'Please have a seat.' He spoke in their native Norwegian. Unsure whether she was annoyed most by the invitation to sit down on her own vessel or by his own failure to stand up, she chose to remain standing. 'How are things?'

The Captain took a long, deep breath. 'Things, inspector, are critical,' she said. 'I'm not sure who will explode first: my crew or my passengers. The flights back to Buenos Aires are scheduled for tomorrow morning and are immovable. We have twenty-four hours in which to deliver a programme for our guests. I'm aware that your investigation of the two deaths is of the utmost importance, but I respectfully request that you allow us to begin that programme with a normal breakfast in the restaurant. While they are breakfasting – and you as well, I trust – my expedition team would very much like to announce the local tour options that they have spent all night organising.'

Harket was silent for several seconds, before he stood up and noisily cleared his throat.

'Very well,' he said. 'Last night Bakke and Bautista packed up all our bits and pieces into boxes. If you could have them moved to a secure room, you may then allow the passengers to leave their cabins – but not the ship – and take breakfast as normal. I will make a decision on disembarkation and wi-fi within an hour. Anything else, Captain?'

'No, inspector,' she said, before forcing out the two words she knew she had to say. 'Thank you. Oh, and you have another visitor waiting outside.'

'Who is it?'

'Mr Pound.'

With that she turned and went briskly about her business, leaving Harket in an unusually good mood. He had, of course, already decided on these actions before the Captain had asked him.

'Come in, Mr Pound!' he called, reverting to English.

Harry entered, closing the door behind him.

'How did you sleep, inspector?' he asked.

'Very well, thank you. And you?

'Not so well.' Harket seemed genuinely concerned. 'I was kept awake by what I call a whirry brain. A number of things occurred to me... leading to a number of other things. You did say I might disturb you if I thought them important.'

'I did. Please sit down and fire at me.'

'Fire away, we say. Well, there are only two really. The first concerns the equipment that poor Dr Dulacki took ashore at Andvord Bay. I understand it's now in the hands of the people at the Chilean naval base.' Harket nodded. 'Well, I'm no meteorologist, but I feel sure that stored in this equipment must be some readings he took before he was, well, attacked – as we assume he was. And these readings must be timed. So surely retrieving this data would tell us what time the perpetrator disturbed him. This in turn, compared with the timed re-entries aboard might serve at least to exclude some guests and crew – and even point the finger at some others.'

Harket had been nodding throughout.

'You're right,' he said. 'I'll get onto it as soon as I can. And the second thing?'

'Well, it's Clemente Gil. You say he's no longer our concern but, well, *I'm* concerned. Couldn't we, shouldn't we be keeping up to date on his progress, his safety? Might you perhaps chase the Chilean police for the latest news?'

'You are psychical, Mr Pound. In my messages this morning was one from the Chief of Police in Punta Arenas, written yesterday. Let me read it to you.' He picked up his phone. 'His English is even worse than mine. Yes, here's the main piece... "In the regarding of the two passengers exited of the *MS Grettis*, after something difficult with the papers the perpetrated Gil he is scheduled to travel tomorrow morning by aeroplane to Arturo Merino Benitez, airport of Santiago. There, he is scheduled to travel by aeroplane to Madrid. The perpetrator Moreno he is disappeared in PA city and is now outside our view."'

'I see. Do you think this is good news or bad news, Inspector?'

'I think it is possibly both, Mr Pound.'

21

Later that morning, Santiago de Chile

'Anywhere. Fast.'

An unusual request, thought the taxi driver, but the customer is always right. Into first, away from the rank and into the lane headed for the city. The city is 'anywhere', right?

'Centre?' he asked, glancing at the mirror. But his passenger was looking through the rear window, rucksack still around his shoulders.

In the queue at departures Clemente Gil had dared to think he'd nearly made it when, just a few places in front, a head turned around. A head he instantly recognised as one of Pepe's foot soldiers. Here on holiday? Just possible. Why in front of me, not behind? Another quick decision needed. The man was approaching passport control, looking forward. Not worth the risk. Gil had walked briskly away. No backward look, into a crowd.

Now in the temporary safety of the taxi, he finally turned away from the window and slumped into the seat. Something crumpled in his back pocket. Pulling out the street map he'd picked up in the arrivals hall, his thoughts drifted back many years to a night in Málaga...

'Quinta Normal.'

The driver was relieved to finally have a destination.

'Park Quinta Normal, sir?'

'Yes.'

*

On a bench in the shade of a eucalyptus tree, looking over a rough patch of grass where children played in the sunshine, Gil felt safer than he had since he'd left Spain. Safety in numbers was normally best, but right now, with his mind in a whirl, what he needed was some peace and quiet. Some space to breath. All the same he did another full three-sixty.

The Chilean capital was new ground to him. Until he'd stepped off the *Grettis* he'd never even set foot in Chile. But in the taxi what had popped into his mind from way back was a time from his days on the beat in Málaga when he'd been called to a bar frequented by British tourists. Drunk as usual, they'd whipped up an argument that was getting out of hand. Basic English was a requirement for that beat and as soon as he'd starting asking the troublemakers about the beer, they were troublemakers no longer. Drunk they might have been, but one young man who became expansive on his drinking travels in South America identified Santiago as the best pint he'd had. El Pub Yungay, he'd said. An English name for a bar eight thousand miles from home. Why the name had stuck in Gil's mind he didn't know, but sure enough there on his map was the district of Yungay and there on his phone was El Pub Yungay. Must be a tourist area, he thought. A plan was taking shape.

After half an hour on the park bench, the plan was fully formed. Walking back to the park entrance, map in hand, pack on back, he looked for all the world like a tourist. Compañia de Jesús wasn't a street exactly swimming with tourists. He walked on. The nearer he got to the address the fewer people were out and about. Maybe this was a mistake. He'd get to the bar anyway. Turn here, one more block. There it was: on the left, a dusty-looking bar, one table with two chairs outside, a roughly painted sign declaring 'Yungay Arms' and beneath, written in an unsteady hand, '*Cervezas Especiales*'. Not a soul in sight. Gil hesitated. This definitely wasn't going to work. A Plan B was needed. Well, a beer would go down well and might even oil the brain cells. He walked through the open door.

The bar was to the left, tables to the right. Just one at the back was occupied. Dropping his pack on the table nearest the bar, he ordered a small local beer and sat facing the bar, now empty. He was looking down at the map as though it might give him an idea when his beer arrived.

'Thank you,' he said looking up. But it wasn't the barman's face he found himself staring at. Above a jacket even more crumpled than usual, it was the face he least wanted to see.

'Hello, Javi,' said Pepe quietly. 'Fancy seeing you here.'

*

Gil made a start for the door, but it was blocked by a tall young man, arms folded. At the other side of the room, the other customers were being hastily led out through the back by the barman. Gil's erstwhile boss had slowly sat down at his table, back to the bar.

'Sit down, Javi.' he said in a calm voice. 'You may as well have your beer.'

Gil did as he was told, but as he reached for the glass, Pepe suddenly brushed it aside, broken glass and beer spreading over the floor. He leaned forward until his face was barely an inch from Gil's.

'You've led us a fine chase, Clemente Gil,' he growled, 'but now the hunt is over. And I think the prey knows it will shortly meet its fate.'

Training, thought Gil. Click in. Never appear intimidated. Keep the subject talking. He leaned back, away from Pepe's foul breath.

'How did you know I'd be here?' he asked in as steady a voice as he could manage.

Pepe also leaned back.

'Call it a long shot.' he said. 'Back in BA, when you were in a chatty mood – which wasn't often – you spoke about this and that. You remember when Santiago came up? You said you knew nothing about it except one bar. When we heard you were in Punta Arenas, Santiago was the logical next step. So young López and I...' He nodded at the hulk still blocking the exit. '... we thought we'd come on a little break. Didn't take you long to end up somewhere familiar.'

Gil had the feeling that, unless he could come up with something quickly, this may be the place he would end up full stop. Caught out by a simple misunderstanding. Looking briefly over at the door, he got a quick glance of someone just outside in the street, someone he'd not normally want to see, but here and now any interruption could be utilised. Had to be utilised. While Pepe developed his theme of treachery, Gil slowly placed his hands under the table in readiness. Whatever happened, this might be his only chance.

As the door crashed open, López lurched forward. Pepe looked round. Gil, head down, lifted the table up. A shot rang out, a cry. By the time a second shot cracked a mirror on the wall, Gil was past it and in the back room. Ignoring the cowering barman as well as the clatters behind, he headed for a door framed by sunlight. Fist on handle. Out. Left. Back gate. Up, over. Breathe. Startled couple. On again, across the road. Calls behind. Ignore, round the corner, main road. A shop, any shop. In.

Back in the bar of El Pub Yungay, the scene of sudden devastation had just as suddenly fallen to an uneasy calm. Silent but for groans from the floor. The first bullet from Luís Moreno's gun, aimed at Gil, had ricocheted off the tabletop and into Pepe's throat. The second, aimed at a now-moving target, missed by a distance. As Pepe had struggled for breath, López tackled the man who'd come from nowhere and shot his boss. By the time López and Moreno stood up, the prey they'd both been hunting was out of the building. While Moreno set off in pursuit, López, mouth hanging open, kneeled beside Pepe.

In the shop, Gil leaned on the counter, panting. Even now, he realised he had only one option left. He stared at the alarmed shopkeeper.

'*Policía?*' said Gil. '*Más próxima?*'

22

Aboard the MS Sturlanga

About the same time that chaos was unfolding two thousand kilometres to the north, Harket, Bakke and Bautista stood calmly observing a stream of passengers disembarking onto the dockside, where they were shepherded onto a line coaches parked alongside. Shepherding was exactly what the Inspector had demanded for the excursions to be allowed: no one to wander off on their own, neither passengers nor crew. With this in mind, their 'incident room' had been moved to a small port-side lounge on Deck Five that had a clear view over the jetty and, beyond, the city of Ushuaia.

'Our murderer is either among those folks off for a coach trip or is still on board,' he said thoughtfully. And then to Bautista: 'Remind me of the names of the two we are to interview, please.'

She looked at her notes.

'Heidi Bräutigam, German, and James Keniston, American,' she said. 'Both members of the Expedition Team.'

'And the cabin card timings?'

'Here they are,' said Bakke. 'I've highlighted the timings for those two and for Dulacki's card.'

'Very good.' He placed this against a second sheet, containing data from Dulacki's equipment, which Harket had already requested before Harry suggested it. Luckily – or unsurprisingly – the personnel at González Videla Base included a trained meteorologist.

'Shall I show Heidi in now, Inspector?'

Harket hesitated.

'Is Mr Pound still aboard?'

Bakke consulted another list.

'No, sir, he's booked out on one of the trips.'

'Hm. Never mind. When the last passenger has boarded the last coach, bring her through.'

*

An hour later, with much needed coffees delivered to their little lounge, the three investigators sat around the table staring at a rather desperate incident board, sipping their drinks in silence. The Inspector spoke.

'What have we learned from the testimonies of Miss Bräutigam and Mr Keniston?'

Bautista was keen to summarise.

'That no one saw – or admits they saw – Dulacki after about 14:15,' she said. 'when Heidi watched him pass by with his equipment. About ten minutes later Heidi handed over to Jimmy, who let no one past during his hour's shift...

'Although some passengers came over to speak to him,' added Bakke.

'Yes. In the meantime Dulacki started taking temperature and humidity readings at precisely 14:34 and continued until the last one at precisely 15:04. Then, at about 15:15, with no reason to know anyone was beyond the last cone – because Heidi forgot to tell him and he was too unobservant to notice the footprints – Jimmy picked up the cone and started to help with the packing up.'

'Until,' continued Bakke, 'about 16:00, when the last tender left with the last boatload of equipment and crew, who registered their

166

cabin cards back on board between 16:10 and 16:24. In the meantime, Dulacki's card had come back on board at 15:15 in among...'

His hesitation allowed Harket to add the crucial but unfortunate information on timings. 'In among,' he said, looking not at the board but at Bakke, 'a group of card numbers all saved in a file with the time 15:15 and only in alphabetical sequence.'

'Er, yes, Inspector. Our systems department is still investigating, but it seems the times are lost. The purpose of the software is simply to match...'

'Never mind, never mind. We have what we have.' Inspector Harket stood up to look out of the window before continuing. 'Only Bräutigam and Keniston appear to have had the opportunity to kill Dulacki. She also has motive, but... but I see no reason why a smart young woman with her life ahead of her would murder a scientist over a simple disagreement about climate change. And Keniston's only connection with Dulacki seems to be that they're both American. Do we think it's either of them?'

But before Bakke or Bautista could offer their opinion a crew member appeared around the corner. He was slightly out of breath. It was Kristoffer Pedersen, the radio operator.

'Message from Scotland Yard, sir,' he panted. All three stared wide-eyed.

'London?' asked Bakke. 'What...'

'Go on,' interrupted the Inspector.

Pedersen spoke in short bursts while checking his notes.

'A concerned man has contacted them... concerned that a British national may have joined this cruise... with the intention of confronting a crew member... over an incident several years ago.' They let him catch his breath. 'The crew member's name is Dulacki. The passenger's name is... Burnet. One T.'

'And do we have a passenger named Burnet with one T?'

Bakke quickly tapped at his screen.

'We do,' he said.

'And where are they?'

Another few taps.

'On Coach B.'

They rushed to the window. The coaches were just beginning to leave the jetty. Bakke tapped into his phone and spoke in rapid Norwegian. A tense few seconds passed before they saw one of the coaches brake sharply.

*

All aboard lurched forward like a co-ordinated dance troupe. A voice came on the coach's loudspeaker, different from the voice that thirty seconds previously had been extolling the delights of their forthcoming jaunt in the hills of Tierra del Fuego.

'I'm sorry, ladies and gentlemen,' she said in English. 'We must wait here for a minute or two. Please remain seated.'

Just as a minute or two turned into five, Nils Bakke and Angel Bautista climbed aboard Coach B. Bakke took the microphone.

'Could Passenger Burnet make herself known please? Danielle Burnet.'

23

Half an hour later

'I'm sorry you're missing your day out, Ms Burnet,' said Harket.

Angel Bautista, sitting beside him, was surprised by the Inspector's soft voice. Without his heavy glasses he seemed a different person. She believed he may even have smiled, but was careful to look only at the interviewee. As this was Bautista's first-ever experience of a police interview – on either side of the table – Inspector Harket had given her a brief lesson on her role: operate the recorder, observe the interviewee, stay silent. After several days of constant motion, either of the vessel or of its occupants, it was almost relaxing sitting here with the sunshine pouring in from the eastern sky. Even Ms Burnet seemed calm.

'It's Mrs, actually,' said Danielle, pushing her long hair off her collar. 'I'm proud to have my late husband's name, but you can call me Danielle if you like.'

Her gentle Scots tones had come to the fore. She sat upright. While Bautista didn't recognise the accent, she recognised the assuredness with which her words were delivered and sensed this lady knew why she was here and may even have been expecting it.

'Had you ever met Dr Ralph Dulacki before this trip, Danielle?' asked Harket.

'No.'

'Did you speak to him during the voyage?'

'Yes, I did. At the end of his talk.'

'May I ask what you discussed?'

'It's no secret. I asked him if he remembered my son.'

Harket held his glasses to glance at his notes.

'Arthur?'

'Yes.'

'I understand he died in Antarctica, at Rothera Station. May I give my condolence, Danielle.'

The odd English brought an unexpected smile from the Scotswoman.

'Thank you, Inspector. Actually Art died just *outside* Rothera Station. Precisely eight hundred metres outside in fact. Cold and alone in the snow. At night.'

Bautista swallowed hard. This was news to her. How could the boy's mother stay so calm?

'A tragedy,' continued Harket. 'A young man with his life before him. And did Dr Dulacki remember him?'

'He did.'

'May I ask how your conversation continued?'

'I pointed out to Dr Dulacki that, although the inquest concluded that Art left the station while the state of his mind was disturbed, the reason for this 'disturbance' was unknown at the time. Since then Art's diaries have been returned to me...' Danielle took a sip of water. 'Inspector, may I tell you about my son?'

'Please do.'

She adjusted her position.

'We had two sons, Joshua and Arthur. They were very different children and I loved – I love – them both equally. When we moved from Scotland to Yorkshire for Bob's job – that's my husband – Josh settled in quickly. He makes friends easily. But Art was a bit of a loner. He was also closest to his father. So when Bob died...'

Bautista's face crinkled a little and Harket was clearly about to give another condolence when Danielle's raised hand stopped him.

'When Bob died,' she continued, 'Art took it hardest, withdrew further into himself and – this may sound a little strange – he seemed to adopt the village's most famous son, Captain Cook, as a replacement father. Captain Cook the explorer.'

'James Cook, yes,' said Harket, nodding. 'We Norwegians are also explorers. Please go on.'

'So Art began to dream about travelling the world. When he applied to Imperial College he told us it was the best course but soon we realised it was just to be in London, near the best museums, the best map shops and of course near to Heathrow. At the end of every term he'd be off somewhere – first Europe, then the US, then the Far East – paid for by term-time jobs. While the other students were at parties or pubs, Art would be earning extra cash, sometimes as a barman at the same pubs. It helped that he lived for free at the little flat Bob had bought down there – the one where I now live in fact. Before Art left uni, he'd set foot on every continent except one.'

While Danielle took another drink, Bautista turned to look at Harket, who, holding up the palm of his hand, signalled they should stay silent.

'So four years ago, when the temporary research post in Antarctica came up, Art jumped at it, flew through the interview and ended up down here. Others would have struggled to be without their friends for so long, but Art didn't really have anyone close. Never did. Just to be in the last wilderness on earth was a dream come true – and to see the things that Cook had seen right here...' She waved her arm at the window, at the Beagle Channel, at Navarino Island beyond. '... well, that was a bonus.'

For a moment or two Danielle seemed lost in the sunlight that bathed her face.

'You were in touch with your son by the internet of course,' prompted Harket.

As she turned back to the table, Bautista noticed a tear running down Danielle's cheek. She wiped it away.

'Yes, he sent long messages to both of us at first, to Josh and me. Video calls too. Art was absolutely in his element. The cold, the dark, he seemed to embrace it all. Loved it. Even made some friends among his colleagues, even a girl. That was unheard of for Art. But then the the the messages got shorter. There were long days when we heard nothing. A week here, a week there. Eventually we got the news.' Another sip of water. 'The news that he'd gone missing. How can you be missing in a tiny cluster of buildings on a little headland cut off from the rest of the world? Then twenty-four hours later, the news that... that he'd been found beyond the fence, in the snow, long dead. Curled up like a baby.'

Bautista broke the silence.

'I'm so sorry,' she whispered, wiping a tear from her own cheek.

'Dr Dulacki was at the inquest, wasn't he?' asked Harket, bringing the three of them back to the point. 'In London.'

'I knew he had no feelings when I listened to him,' said Danielle. 'Diligent scientist, he said about Art. Exemplary member of staff, well-liked. All phrases out of a text book. He didn't really know my son at all.'

'Should he have done?'

Danielle suddenly leaned across the table, eyes wide.

'He was Art's mentor, for Christ's sake!' she snapped at Harket. 'He was supposed to keep an eye on him, listen to him. He was supposed to be looking after my son! Instead he was poisoning his mind with his wild ideas.'

Harket leaned back in his chair, genuine confusion on his face.

'What wild ideas? Was it something in Arthur's diaries?'

Danielle also leaned back.

'You weren't at Dulacki's lecture, were you, Inspector? What about you, Angel?'

Bautista checked with Harket before replying.

'No, Danielle,' she said. 'We don't have time to listen to lectures.'

'Well,' continued Danielle, 'it's climate change. This climate emergency, as we're now supposed to call it.'

'Surely these aren't wild ideas,' said Harket. 'Did your son disagree? He was a scientist after all.'

'It's not climate change itself, Inspector. No one in their right minds denies that. It's the guilt. That's all Dulacki talked about in his lecture and that's what he filled my son's head with. International travel: guilty. Flying for pleasure: guilty. Cruise ships: guilty. Guilt, guilt, guilt. My son was a sensitive boy. He liked to act like he could survive anything, but he was still that lonely little boy who needed a father. When the one man who was supposed to be filling that role, protecting him, told him we're all to blame, he just seems to have taken it all on himself. That's why Art stopped writing to us. That's why he stole the keys to the gate and walked out of that place one night and... and...'

'... died cold and alone in the snow,' completed Harket, before leaning forward once more. 'Like Ralph Dulacki.'

Bautista noticed that Danielle looked genuinely surprised. But for a moment Harket's attention was on the door where one of the young receptionists stood poised to knock. When she did, Harket couldn't hide his irritation. Without waiting for an invitation, she entered and handed a sheet of paper to Bautista.

'What you asked for, Angel,' she whispered. After adding 'Sorry, sir', she quickly departed, leaving the room enveloped in a tense silence.

Bautista quickly glanced at the paper before passing it to Harket, her finger poking at the line highlighted in felt tip at the bottom. He put on his glasses and for a moment or two remained motionless, simply staring at the sheet, and then looked up at Danielle. It was Danielle who broke the silence.

'He deserved it,' she said, no emotion in her voice. 'We'd all guessed he died. I'm glad it was like that. I admit it. But if you think I killed him, you need to know...'

'… that you didn't go ashore at Andvord Island,' said Harket, removing his glasses and tapping them on the sheet.'

'No.'

'What did you do?'

'I sat here on board with an American woman, Maisie, watching her sketch. She's very good.'

Harket leaned on the table, slowly stroking his chin, before looking up once again at his interviewee.

'Before you started the story of your two sons, Danielle, you were telling us about your discussion with Dr Dulacki after his lecture.'

'Yes.'

'How did it develop?'

'I challenged him about his attitude to Arthur, about this, this... accusation of guilt that had such an impact on him. I asked him if he knew what effect it had – and if he felt any guilt himself about Art's death.'

'And did he?'

'Not a drop. He said their job as physical scientists was to identify cause and effect in the environment, not in humans. That was the job of psychologists, experts in mental health. It wasn't his field, he said.'

Bautista shook her head.

'And how did you react?'

'I walked away.'

'Even though you must have been angry inside.'

'Fuming.

Once again Harket stroked his chin and looked down at the table before raising his eyes. Head at a quizzical angle, he asked one more question.

'Danielle, was anyone with you at the lecture?'

24

The same morning, a few miles inland

It had been ten years since Jesús Padrón began shooting beavers. He still culled one or two from time to time, but the battle, he'd decided, had been lost. These odd ones were just for food. Stir-fried beaver meat was surprisingly tender and went down well with the tourists who drove up to his little wooden café in the woods. Even better with those who'd worked up an appetite walking the mountainous trails of eastern Tierra del Fuego.

Back in the 1940s these semi-aquatic rodents were supposed to bring money to this poor region. In what was thought to be a brainwave, the Argentinian authorities brought just ten pairs of Canadian beavers all the way from Manitoba to the this southernmost tip of Patagonia, the idea being that they would multiply and their valuable fur would bring in hunters, traders, settlers – in a word, money. Over the intervening seventy years they'd multiplied all right, but what they'd actually brought was chaos. Damming watercourses, diverting rivers, creating lakes where none had existed, the little creatures had thrived – while the rest of the ecosystem slowly collapsed. Getting a gun licence to help try and rid the island of what had become vermin was easy. Curbing the beavers' numbers was harder. In the end, Jesús had given up, setting up a hospitality business to make what he could from a devastated landscape which, for whatever reason, tourists seemed to find – if not exactly attractive, at least worth a visit. Casa Jesús was now beginning to show a profit and there was no way he'd turn down the two coachloads he was offered by the Ushuaia tourist office, even if it was with less than twenty-four hours' notice. Slapping another beaver carcass down on the work surface, he was pleased to see through the kitchen window the two vehicles rumble down the rough track from Highway 3 and into his car park.

*

As Coach B squeezed through the busy streets of Ushuaia, some slightly bewildered faces stared from its windows at the sight of traffics, shops and people without standard-issue waterproofs. Harry had been two rows behind Fiona and Danielle when they'd all lurched forward and eventually the latter had been escorted from the bus. By the time they were heading east on the main road out of the straggling conurbation of Ushuaia and no one had filled the vacant seat, Harry's social conscience got the better of him.

'Do you mind if I join you?' he asked Fiona.

She'd been staring at the dark green landscape that had begun to unfold under heavy grey skies and jumped a little.

'Oh, it's you, she said, 'Er no, help yourself.'

Squashing himself into a seat that, like almost all coach seats, was too small for his frame, he asked the obvious question.

'Do you know why Danielle went back to the ship?'

'No,' she said. 'No idea. I hope no one's died. The poor girl's had enough to put up with.'

With no elaboration forthcoming, Harry decided to get straight to the reason he'd changed seats.

'Look, Fiona, I'm sorry for our little argument the other day. I was out of order. I shouldn't have got angry with you – it's just that some things irritate me and I should learn to keep them to myself.' His mind briefly flicked back to Louise telling him exactly that.

'Oh, no bother, Harry. There's plenty in the world to irritate us all a hundred times over, isn't there? Keeping the peace isn't that easy.' She paused, turning back to the window. 'But the Lord tells us to try all the same. You know, I thought this Terror di Fuego would be, well, terrifying like it sounds, but it's as soft and green as Ireland. And just as wet.'

Indeed it had started to rain. After a few banal comments about the weather, they fell into an uncomfortable silence that lasted until they turned off at the 'Casa Jesús' sign.

'Well, here we are, Harry,' she said with a sigh, as if coming out of a daydream.

'Time for a little exercise, I'm told,' said Harry.

At the end of the bumpy track, as they rose from their seats and shuffled down the coach, Harry decided he'd leave Fiona to make her own way around the trail or join another group. It had been easier to make his peace than he'd thought. What might have prompted this new, withdrawn Fiona he didn't know. Maybe the end of the trip. Whatever it was, the new version was certainly less exhausting than the old one.

*

Nils Bakke stood to one side, observing closely while the passengers stepped down from both buses. Having delivered Danielle Burnet to Harket, he'd been expecting to sit in on the interview but the inspector had asked him to hurry back to the line of coaches, headed out on different day trips, and take a position in one of them as an extra security presence. There'd been only one coach where he knew for certain there was a free seat, but on boarding he'd found another one next to the tour guide.

With all safely counted off, he tried to send a message back to the

Sturlanga to confirm their arrival but, with no signal out here in the wilds and no wi-fi till they got to the restaurant, he had to give up and hurried to join the back of the large, straggling group as it set off on the hour-long hike in the hills promised by the guide. Just ahead of him he spotted Harry and quickened his pace to join him.

'Hey, Harry,' he called, momentarily looking away from the muddy path. As Harry turned, Bakke's feet slipped away from him and he tumbled sideways onto a log. A volley of indecipherable Norwegian echoed through the trees, ending with the internationally understood 'Ow... aieee!'.

Harry hurried back.

'Nils, are you all right?'

'It's these shoes. Didn't have time to get the right boots for a walk. No, Harry, I'm... owaiee!... not all right. Think I've twisted an uncle.'

This wasn't the time to correct the Security Officer's English.

'Can I help you up?' asked Harry.

Bakke looked at the line of people disappearing into the distance.

'No, no. Look. I'll get back to the bus, but can you please stay with the group? The guide's at the front. If you stay at the back, you'll keep all of them together. He's got the numbers.'

'Yes, of course. If you're sure you'll be OK.'

As he headed off, Bakke called after him.

'It's important, Harry.'

'OK. Don't worry.'

*

While the little Canadian invaders had transformed the valley bottom into a meandering maze of pools, the slopes above remained untouched and were mostly covered by conifers or by beech trees just beginning to lose their leaves in the southern autumn. After a week or more of nothing but the black and white of bare rock and snow drifts, Harry was somehow relieved to see that the rest of the Earth was still going about its luxuriant seasonal business. It was even a relief simply to feel grass and soil under his feet. As the path rose higher, one or two bare patches appeared and at one of these the whole group had been brought to a halt by the guide, who'd found the highest rock from which addressed the assembly.

'Please stay on that side of me,' he started, 'as behind me is a steep drop to the valley floor. Now, up here we see the southernmost conifer in the world, *Pilgerodendron uviferum*. Yes, those tall, narrow trees over there...'

For someone who himself frequently talked to large groups of tourists, Harry wasn't the best at standing still to listen to someone else and instead sat to the side on a small log, daydreaming. The end of the trip wasn't far off, he thought. Tomorrow he'd be on the plane back to Buenos Aires and then on to London. It seemed a bit surreal to think that, while they'd all been chugging around in the vast wilderness of Antarctica, the rest of the world, with its traffic, its factories and all its day-to-day pre-occupations, had just been carrying on as normal. Before all that he'd need to check in with Inspector Harket when he got back on board the *Sturlanga*, find out if he'd made any headway in his investigations and make one last effort to get news about the fate of Clemente Gil. With these thoughts whirring around in his head, he'd completely failed to notice the guide had stopped talking and the stragglers of the group were already almost out of sight among the trees.

Hastily pushing himself to his feet, he was just setting off after them, when he heard a strange sound to his left. It sounded like some kind of murmuring. And yet no one was to be seen. After walking around in bemusement, he finally noticed one of the ship's green waterproofs – not designed for this landscape – on the other side of the clearing. He was looking at the person's back.

'Hey, hi!' he called. Hurrying towards the figure, he realised they were on the edge of the precipice. 'Hey there, come away! It's dangerous.' As he approached, Harry recognised, over the coat's collar, some familiar curls.

Fiona slowly turned round.

'Stay away,' she said, before turning back towards the drop and resuming her prayers.

'Fiona, it's Harry. What are you doing? Come away, please.'

'I said stop. Stay there.'

Harry pulled up. He could now close enough to see the string of pools far below, interspersed with the strange, ghostly-white trunks of trees killed by the rising waters.

'Fiona, what on earth's going on?'

Very slowly she turned to face him, bare heels within inches of the cliff edge.

'We must all pay for our sins, Harry. The Lord God knows all our ways, all our thoughts, all our actions.'

'What sins, what actions?'

'The evil doctor has paid. And now it's my turn.'

She backed even closer to the edge. Harry stepped forward.

'No!' he shouted. 'Fiona, no, no...'

Staring straight into his eyes, she resumed her murmuring.

'Forgive me, father, for I have...'

But of her final prayer no more was heard, as Fiona Phelan disappeared from view.

PART

FOUR

RETURN

25

That evening

The Panorama Lounge was full for the Captain's Farewell. Most held glasses of sparkling wine. Once again Lennox Montgomery was standing near the back, this time with Maisie for company and Vernon Jennings for what Lennox knew would be supplementary information, invited or not. Of the Usual Suspects, three were missing this evening.

Lennox sighed.

'I know where poor Fiona is,' he said quietly. The whole ship probably knew. No official announcement had been made, but on any vessel news carries fast. 'And I guess Dani's helping sort out arrangements. But where's Harry? Anyone heard?'

The question was as much for all within earshot as for Vernon, but of course the font of all knowledge was happy to oblige.

'He'll be at the local police station,' he said. 'I saw Nils and that detective being picked up by a police car earlier on. I guess there's a lot to sort out. By the way, Nils was limping. Don't know whether there was some kind of a struggle.'

'I heard on the grapevine,' said Maisie, gulping a little, 'there's nobody could've saved her. Only Harry was there. Say, do you think we should put in a good word for him? Could be he's in trouble.'

'That's a kind thought, honey,' said Lennox, placing a gentle arm around his wife. 'We'll see if we can catch the Captain later on – hey, there she is. Shush, everyone.'

Captain Thommessen stepped up to the stage. The powerful presence that had held the attention of those present at the Welcome Address was gone. In its place was a picture of sadness, almost of defeat. Hunched slightly, she accepted the microphone from Stefan and turned to look at her audience, eyes a little unfocussed. The room fell into silence.

'Ladies and gentlemen,' she began, before a long pause. No one moved. 'Ladies and gentlemen, this has been a difficult voyage for all of us. Usually at this point, I recall the highlights of the week, the adventures both here on board and of course ashore on the edge of the world's most magical continent. And, yes, there have been some good times. But this is not the time to remember them. This is the time to remember the three people who set sail with us from this very dockside eight days ago, but who will not be returning home.'

By now Maisie was sobbing. She wasn't the only one.

'I speak.' the Captain continued, 'of our guests Joseph Challinor and Fiona Phelan and of our fellow crew member Ralph Dulacki.' Lennox noticed she didn't refer to any notes. 'They were all someone's family member, someone's friend. As we silently raise our glasses to the dear departed, our thoughts go not only to them but to those who will miss them To the dear departed.'

And silently raise their glasses everyone did, even those who'd heard the rumour that one of the dear departed may have been responsible for the departure of another one. Several at one side of the lounge turned their raised glasses towards Karen Challinor, who they noticed had bravely joined in with many of the activities just days after her husband's disappearance. After a long pause, Captain Thommessen resumed.

'And finally may I offer my personal thanks to every one of my crew – maritime crew, expedition crew and hotel staff – for their incredible hard work in very trying circumstances. And to all of you, our guests, for your patience and understanding in what was probably not quite the voyage you – or any of us – was expecting. I do hope we might see you again on our cruise line, perhaps on this very vessel. Our expedition crew and I will be staying here in the lounge for a while if you have any questions you'd like to ask us. Stefan will now take the microphone to explain the arrangements for tomorrow morning. Thank you.'

A ripple of polite applause accompanied the Captain off the stage. Even while the Expedition Team Leader began to speak, a queue had begun to form near her. She knew without hearing even the first question that most would be about one subject: compensation.

*

As the farewell gathering began to break up, a car was making its way from the office of the Ushuaia's Provincial Police Commissioner through the dusty suburbs towards the port. Next to the uniformed driver sat Nils Bakke, his heavily bandaged leg stretched before him. Behind sat Detective Inspector Jakob Harket and Hieronymus Pound.

'I didn't know anyone was watching,' said Harry. 'I thought Fiona and I were on that clifftop alone.'

Bakke turned to answer.

'I succeeded to get enough statements from the looker-ons to convince the Commissioner you did all you could to stop her.'

'This is in no way a success, Bakke. Not for the British police in London, not for me on the *Sturlanga* and not for you in the field.' Harry didn't know whether this breast-beating was for his benefit or not. 'The Metropolitan Police in London took thirty-six hours – thirty-six hours in this day of the age! – to get a message to the *MS Sturlanga* that we had a passenger with probable bad intention.'

Harry barely had the energy even to notice the poor English, and anyway had recently come to realise many things were more important. 'And I... I have failed to do anything near a proper background check on Dulacki. The incident three years ago, the inquest... it was all there online if I had had the wit... is it called wit, Mr Pound?'

'Yes,' said Harry, turning towards the Inspector, 'wit, intelligence, sharpness...' he trailed off as, in the darkness of the car, Harket returned his stare.

'The wit to look for it. And Bakke, you are a senior Security Officer and yet you wear the shoes of... of a ballroom dancer! In the mountains of Tierra del Fuego!'

'But...' started Bakke.

Harket's theatrical sigh cut off his excuse.

'This is a disaster for all of us. Oh, except for you, Mr Pound. You have been put in a difficult position yet again and behaved with honour.'

'And a disaster for poor Fiona,' said Harry quietly. He already knew the image of the Irishwoman's last few seconds would never leave him. 'Inspector, are you absolutely sure she did it because it was her that had... had done for Dr Dulacki.'

'I tell you, Mr Pound, because I know you can keep this to yourself. The local police found a note the deceased left in her bag on the coach and Bakke here translated it for them. How did you describe it, Bakke?'

'It was very... very rambling – I think this is the word in English. More a confession in the Catholic sense than in the criminal sense. But her reference to Dulacki was very clear.'

'Are you sure it was her writing?' asked Harry. He was clutching at straws.

'Not *absolutely* sure, to use your phrase, Mr Pound,' said Harket.

'I admit we would benefit from some hard evidence. And we are working on that. The suicide in the hills is a case for the Argentinian police, but the Dulacki case is for the Norwegian police service. And I shall not fail.'

'But *I* have failed,' insisted Harry. 'I tried to save her. And failed. It's happened again.'

*

As the three of them re-boarded the *Sturlanga* at Deck Five's security check, in a gesture that surprised Harry, Inspector Harket held out his hand to help the limping Bakke off the steps. In doing so, he dropped his glasses and in an awkward moment fumbled around beneath the scanner as Bakke and then Harry scanned their cabin cards. Walking towards the lift, Harket turned to the others.

'We have just proved how Ms Phelan beat the computer,' he said. Bakke and Harry looked at him. 'In creating some innocent confusion, we scanned only two cards. How easy it must have been for an unstable lady of a certain age to have likewise distracted the crew and scanned two instead of one.'

'But I scanned mine,' said Bakke.

'And I mine,' said Harry.

'But not I,' said Harket. With a spring in his step, he walked back to the scanner, apologised and beeped himself back aboard. The Inspector was back on form.

As Harry set off towards his cabin for a much-needed shower, he turned back to Harket.

'Inspector,' he said, 'while we're clearing up loose ends, at Andvord Bay how did Fiona get to and from Dulacki without being seen?'

'Ah,' replied Harket before heading to the lift. 'I asked that very question to those at the naval base. They have been very helpful to us. Maybe they have nothing much else to do, but they volunteered to go back and inspect the crime scene again. It turns out there's a very easy walking route around the other side of a little hillock that would avoid the two crew members by the cone. All that was stopping anyone using it was a flimsy rope marking the edge of the permitted path. I think that would hardly stop someone with murder in mind. Anything else?'

'Yes, since you ask. How on earth does a small woman in her sixties overcome a bigger, fitter and younger man? Not only overcome him but knock him unconscious?'

'Mr Pound, you have identified the elephant in the china shop. I think I know the answer, but hope to have confirmation later. I believe the bar has re-opened. Will you be there later?'

26

'I knew she was angry,' said Danielle between sobs, 'but how could she be more angry than me? He was my son, not hers.'

Maisie sighed. 'For us Christians,' she said, 'the power of faith can be stronger than emotion.'

They were sitting in Danielle's cabin, among the part-packed cases, half of which belonged to her friend. She looked around and once again began to cry.

'And I've got to pack all this stuff too,' she mumbled. 'How can I get it all back? Maisie, I don't know what I'm doing any more.'

'Honey, you just pack your own stuff. I'll do the rest. And anyway, didn't you say they'll move it all to your hotel in town for you tomorrow? I guess they'll handle poor Fi's things themselves. Look, why don't we both take a break and...'

There was a gentle knock at the door. Maisie answered it, listened to the steward and turned back to Danielle.

'They say they want Fiona's water bottle. Do you know which is hers?'

*

Deck Eight was awash with passengers spilling from the restaurant, many in elegant outfits more suited to a Caribbean cruise than one self-consciously branded as an 'expedition'.

'Where have all these people come from?' Harry asked Lennox.

They were standing at the bar. The American was among the more formally dressed, and even Harry had reluctantly pulled out his one and only tie. 'There are some I've never seen before.'

'Oh, they've been in their cabins,' said Lennox, 'or their suites. Surprised us too on our first cruise. You know, Harry, I'll bet for some of these folks it's their second or third time down to Antarctica. Seen one penguin, seen 'em all, I guess. Hey, there's Maisie, Over here, honey! And she's got Dani with her. Looks like she needs a drink even more than you, buddy. Vernon's kept that table in the corner. If you get the girls over there, I'll follow with the drinks.'

Before they sat down, Harry and even Vernon gave Danielle a big hug. Harry was relieved the focus wasn't all on him. His day had been tough enough, but Danielle's had undoubtedly been worse. Maisie, who seemed to have taken on the role of mother hen, had firmly her placed next to herself on the sofa. After an awkward silence in which no one seemed to know what to say to Danielle, it was Harry who broke the ice.

'Have you spoken to your son, Dani?' he asked quietly. He'd heard from Harket about the tip-off from London.

Danielle nodded.

'What about Fiona's family?' asked Vernon. 'Have they been told?'

Danielle stared at the floor. Her shoulders were shaking. Maisie was beginning to think coming to the bar had been a mistake. Where was her husband with those drinks?

'Dani doesn't know much about Fi's family,' Maisie explained. But Danielle raised her head.

'I didn't even know the name Nils showed me on her next-of-kin form,' she said. 'It was an address in Ireland. I only knew her through the book club. In fact I hardly knew Fiona at all. I asked her to come on the cruise with me because I didn't want to be on my own. And, well, I thought she was the sort of person who'd draw attention away from me.'

'You were right enough there,' said Vernon and a sad sort of laughter rippled around the group as Lennox appeared with the tray of drinks. And with a young woman in a check shirt.

'There you are, honey,' said Maisie. 'And, my, it's Heidi, ain't it? Haven't seen you around for days. You joining us?'

'Hello, everyone,' said the German, flashing a bright smile that just as quickly disappeared. 'Oh, and I'm very sorry to hear about your friend. It's awful.'

'I'd heard you were confined to quarters,' said Vernon.

'Well, I've been released. Like everyone else.'

'*Are* you joining us?' asked Vernon, ostentatiously making space next to him.

'Actually,' said Lennox, after distributing the drinks, 'Heidi asked if she might have a quick word with Danielle. In private.'

Seeing an escape route, Danielle quickly agreed and, taking her wine, walked off with the German. Shortly after, Harry also had to make his excuses, as Inspector Harket, hardly someone any expected in the bar – and still something of a *persona non grata* after his draconian restrictions on the passengers – beckoned to the Englishman.

'Yes, Inspector,' said Harry, now somewhat recovered with a drink inside him, 'what can I do for you?'

'You've done quite enough for us all, Mr Pound. No, it is I that have news for you. First – and I tell you this on the understanding that it does not go beyond us' Harry nodded. 'We have found a match between a substance with anaesthetic properties found in Dulacki's stomach – a proper post-mortem has finally taken place – and traces of the same substance remaining in Ms Phelan's water bottle.'

'You mean those bottles we were all issued with?'

'Yes.'

'So he was drugged?'

'Yes. It was a possibility I had in mind for some time. It removes, so to speak, the elephant...'

'... from the room.' Harry nodded sagely, as though he'd already thought of this. 'Where did she get that kind of drug from?'

Harket shrugged.

'Bautista looked up some records for me. One or two items from the medical room seem to be unaccounted for. Ms Phelan visited the doctor there a few days ago – and Ms Burnet told us she believed her friend's late husband was a pharmacist. Just coincidences maybe.'

'Hm. And the second item?'

'I have received a message from the Chilean police, via the Argentinian police via my office in Buenos Aires – how can there be so many police forces involved?' Harry left this unanswered. 'That your friend Mr Gil has handed himself in to the Santiago police in connection with a murder on their... their patch?'

'Yes, their patch,' he said. 'Clemente has murdered someone?'

'I cannot speak clearly on the matter. But the important information is that Clemente Gil is booked on a flight to Madrid tomorrow morning *under police escort*. More than this I know not.'

Harry let out a long, slow sigh.

'Will we know if he arrives safely?'

'That I cannot tell you, Mr Pound. With all the jurisdictions my head is already in a... in a buzz?'

'In a buzz will do. All our heads are in a buzz today. I can't thank you enough, Inspector Harken.'

They shook hands and after a long day Harken retired to his cabin.

While Harry would have loved to do the same, he knew in the back of his mind that, before the rush of departure in the morning, he had one more person to seek out.

*

Meanwhile, back in the bar, Danielle had returned to boost the Usual Suspects' numbers back up to four. The others were pleased to see that the cloud that had understandably hung over her was beginning to clear.

'Can I buy you all a drink?' she asked. With Vernon, Lennox and Maisie in full – if surprised – agreement, she beckoned the waiter over. 'No Harry?'

'Off on police business,' said Vernon. 'Are we sure he's not a cop?'

'I'll owe him one then.'

'Feeling a little better?' asked Maisie.

'I am,' said Danielle. 'I've just been speaking to my son's girlfriend. Goodness, I never thought I'd say that.'

'Arthur had a girlfriend?' asked Maisie.

'In his diaries from Antarctica Arthur referred to a girl on the base, not naming her of course, and I did begin to wonder. Well, it turns out it was none other than Heidi Bräutigam. More or less straight from university, like Art, she landed a temporary posting at Rothera Research Station and they seemed to hit it off. When he was found... out there... she was devastated. She knew all about Dulacki's brutality, but no one would listen to her. Well, when she got this job and found he filled in here as well, she thought of resigning straight away. But in the end decided to stay on and take on him and his ideas whenever he could. Well, as we've all seen. She said it was as a kind of tribute to Arthur.' Danielle wiped her eyes before going on. 'I came down here to Antarctica to feel near my son. Heidi's made me feel closer than ever. For a moment I was down there with him, comforting him. Protecting him, like I should have.'

*

Harry found Captain Thommessen doing her duties by mixing with the passengers in the bar. When she spotted him hovering in the melée, she made her excuses and beckoned him through to the Panorama Lounge where things were quieter. They found a table for two with a view through the double-deck windows and over the bow to the calm waters of the port. Beyond, the sun was setting over the mountains. They placed their drinks on the table – red wine for him, sparkling water for her.

'You must be exhausted, Captain,' said Harry.

'Ulrika, Harry.'

'And you must be glad this cruise is over... Ulrika.'

'Not just the cruise but the season. This was the last before the ice gets too hazardous. Well, when we dock at the end of every voyage I'm a little sad it's over, but yes, this one... was different.' She raised her glass to him. Harry let her go on. 'Almost always we return with the same passengers and crew we set sail with – well, for a ship's captain that's sort of priority number one! This time I've almost lost count.' She paused. 'There was one man overboard...'

'Probably.'

'Suicide.'

'Possibly.'

'One late-arriving passenger left early, with one crew member.'

'In pursuit.'

'Yes, I heard about the fight in Santiago. Is Moreno arrested? Dead?'

Harry shrugged.

'I'm not the police.'

'No,' she acknowledged, with a sudden wide smile, 'I forget. One deceased crew member...

'Murdered.'

'... and now one deceased passenger..'

'Suicide. 'I make that a net result of minus four. A record?'

The Captain laughed.

'For the cruise line probably. I've got an appointment with the board in Oslo next week.'

'Will there be... a problem?'

'Will they fire me, do you mean? Maybe they won't have to.' Harry turned to look at her. She was staring out to sea. 'Maybe I've done enough of this. Maybe there's a twelve-metre yacht in the Caribbean waiting for a skipper.' She turned back. 'Anyway, what about you, Harry? You didn't come on an Antarctic cruise just to listen to accents and help people with their English. Did you get what you wanted out of it, despite your... your...'

'Adventures? Well, to be honest, Ulrika, I don't know why I came. My friends back home could tell you the reason why *they* said I should come.'

'To find a nice woman to organise my life.'

'Ha! And did you find one, Harry?'

With some effort he avoided her eyes.

'Actually,' he said, 'I lost one.'

She left him time to expand, but it was soon filled by Maria arriving to tell her she was required on the bridge and so Harry and Ulrika parted with a short smile – and a handshake that lingered perhaps a fraction longer than either expected.

27

Following morning

Final disembarkation was another routine aboard the *MS Sturlanga* organised like clockwork around groupings. With none of his friends sharing the Blue Iceberg designation, Harry had said his farewells to them the previous evening, just in case their paths didn't cross at the airport and on the flight. So today after breakfast he found himself, as instructed by loudspeaker, sitting quietly in a lounge with other Icebergs. Quietly enough to hear some Yellow Glaciers chatting as they queued at the final security check, including a voice he half-recognised. Surely that was Vernon – but once again with the refined tones he'd last heard out on Deck Nine five days before.

He hurried out and peered along the line until he spotted that unmistakeable comb-over. Aware he may be about to make a complete fool of himself, Harry hung back to double-check who was speaking. By the time he was certain, Vernon was almost at the gate.

'Vernon!' he called. 'Thought it was you. Bye bye, old chap.'

Vernon turned and, after barely a second in which he clearly realised he'd been caught out, replied with a smile.

'Yes, indeed – old chap. I bet you're wondering if I'm doing an impersonation.' Those around him looked a little bemused.

'Well, are you?'

'My life's an impersonation, Harry. At least life aboard.' Harry joined the bemused. 'Didn't I mention I'm a jobbing actor? Must have slipped my mind. On a cruise you can be anyone you want – just for the duration of course. This is where I practise my trade. You're the expert on accents, old fruit. How am I doing?'

Vernon had been talking over his shoulder as he handed over his cabin card and picked up his hand luggage from the scanner.

'Sounds convincing,' admitted Harry. 'Which is the real one? The one with the Usual Suspects or this one?'

'Ain't neither, dude,' replied Vernon, switching in an instant to urban American. 'Me, I was raised in da Bronx!'

And with that, Vernon Jennings disappeared into the bright sunshine at the end of the world, clenched fist raised to the skies. Harry shook his head. On this trip, he thought, there was bound to be one last surprise.

But the last it was not.

*

If the people and traffic of Ushuaia had felt odd to travellers from Antarctica, the mayhem of Buenos Aires took their disorientation to another level. While the calm blue waters of the Río de la Plata washed the shore barely a hundred metres away, the bus and taxi zone of Jorge Newbery airport could barely cope with wave after wave of passengers spilling from the arrivals hall. Banners and placards competed for attention. Hotel Emperador! City shuttle! *Sr/Sra Gonzalez!* Multi-lingual calls pierced the heavy air. *Aquí aquí!* Next taxi here! Best price!

A large contingent – with rattling wheelie-cases in tow – headed for the stop marked 'Airport Transfer' for the cross-town ride to Ezeiza International. In amongst them, pulling his modest case, was Hieronymus Pound. Harry's height, though, gave him a good view of the various inter-weaving lines of travellers. Close by was the front of the taxi rank, where prospective passengers jostled for the next cab, and it was here that something caught his eye. A flash of red and cream. Where had he seen that before?

Of course. So entangled had he become in other matters, he'd entirely forgotten about straw-hat man. He must have been one of those who'd spent most of the voyage in his cabin, thought Harry. And the test match! Swerving out of his queue, Harry got to the taxi just as the man was telling the driver his destination.

'Hellooo!,' called Harry. 'Who won the test?'

Bending his tall frame into the back seat, the man turned, a little startled. As was Harry.

'Oh, sorry,' said Harry, holding his hand palm up. 'Thought you were someone else. Er, *lo siento, pensé que era otra persona.*'

'Soraight,' said the other, nodding.

The taxi pulled away.

Just before the door had closed, Harry caught a glimpse of the man's companion in the back seat. He stood watching the car move away into the distance. Other passengers bustled past, brushing Harry's elbows. The tall Englishman, however, stood stock still.

*

Eventually Harry turned away and, without conscious intent, let his original queue sweep him up and into the bus. The first half of the journey he spent still processing what he'd seen and heard. What did the man tell the driver? It sounded like 'the colony'. What colony? The second half he spent figuring out what to do. He had to tell someone. But this was a huge city with other matters on its mind. And anyway, would an explanation on the phone – half English, half Spanish – make any sense to anyone? Still in a quandary, he found himself swept off the bus at Ezeiza, re-united with his luggage and standing in another queue at check-in for the Heathrow flight. He felt for his phone, reassured himself there was a signal and found the name of the only person to whom his story would not sound like utter madness. Yes, there it was: Harket, Inspector.

*

From Buenos Aires Ezeiza to London Heathrow is a thirteen-hour flight and most passengers on this particular one were thankful it was overnight. These included Harry, who also gave thanks to a non-existent god that, with the neighbouring seat vacant, he was able to curl some of his frame into at least a diagonal orientation and pass most of the dark hours in a state not dissimilar to sleep.

Although the passengers queueing for passport control at Heathrow were calm, their phones were not. After a dozen beeps around him, Harry gave in to the urge and switched his own on. Just one email – and a welcome one. The sender's name was Gil.

Hola Harry

Ya estoy de nuevo en España! Actually I am on a train nearly in Málaga and find just some minutes to send this message of thanks to my friend who has helped me big to escape from one side of the world to the other. Since I left you on the board of Sturlanga I will not say my route to home has been – I think you say smooth. No, very the contrary. But here I am nearly at home and safe. I think safe. I hope the danger has left you also and that I did not make bad your holiday cruise. If you ever come to Spain you will find a welcome in Andalucía.

Saludos

Clemente

Raising his eyes to the ceiling, Harry let out a long, slow breath. Not smooth indeed. Like his own 'holiday cruise'.

With no one to meet him, he took the opportunity to luxuriate in one of Terminal 3's cafés, legs stretched out before him, cappuccino and cinnamon whirl to hand. It felt strange to be back in a version of England without Louise. As one friend returned to the safety of

Soaiun, he thought, another had met only danger there. To distract himself, he'd bought a morning newspaper at the kiosk. First task was to check the previous day's scorecard from what was by now the second test – but he didn't make it to the sports pages. Instead his gaze fixed on a short headline in the Stop Press column on the front page:

British couple arrested in Uruguay

Below, it referred the reader to the online version of the paper for the details. Uruguay? Maybe. Harry fired up his mobile phone again and after a battle both with innumerable beeps welcoming him to the UK and with his own unfamiliarity with this weird way to read the news, managed to find the following news story.

A couple from Lancashire have been arrested in the South American country of Uruguay on suspicion of murder.

The pair, named by the local police as Joseph Challinor, 56, and Karen Challinor, 55, both of Chorley, had recently been on a cruising holiday in Antarctica and were detained yesterday evening on disembarking from a ferry in the small town of La Colonia, 150 kilometres from the capital Montevideo. It is believed they had travelled from Buenos Aires, Argentina.

'Señor Challinor was travelling under the name of another UK citizen,' Police Chief Lorenzo Pereira told reporters. 'We thank the police forces of Argentina, the UK and Norway for their co-operation in this matter.' The name of the other UK citizen was withheld until their family has been contacted.

As Harry sat back to digest this news, elsewhere in the same terminal a woman in her thirties sat looking at her watch. After hurrying to make it to Heathrow in time, Jacqueline Pennyman had now been waiting for over an hour for a father. At this rate he'd miss the cricket highlights he'd told her he was planning to watch when she'd dropped him off two weeks before.

Fed and watered, Harry finally walked down to the Tube for the train into town and then out again to Gloucestershire. He'd worked out most of what must have happened, but still one thing didn't fit and he'd had to file it for the moment in a mental drawer marked 'One coincidence too far'. On the train he reluctantly investigated some of the beeps on his phone. One from Sami, one from... oh, Inspector Harket. He opened the message.

Dear Mr Pound

So once again you find yourself in the spot and the time. I hope you had a satisfactory flight to London.

To cut short a long story, I have shared your information with the correct authorities and am now in my BA office after returning on the ferry from la Colonia in Uruguay. The Uruguayan police have asked me to sit inside the interviews with the two British people. Because you have made all this possible, I feel justified in sharing with you these... may I call them the 'headlines'?

Yes, you were correct: the two are Mr and Mrs Challinor. The British police tell us that Mr Challinor is known by them. He was part of a gang arrested for a crime (I do not know which) several years ago, but his prison sentence was shorter than the others because he assisted the investigation. Since his former friends have been released, he has been in fear for his life – or this he says – and so he was desperate to escape with his wife. In a bar in London they had a piece of luck. They saw a man with similar height and – how do you say it? – similar looks to Mr Challinor and they formed a plan. All this they have now admitted. They returned to the same bar on several nights and listened to the man in conversation with his friends. Here they learned he will take a cruise in Antarctica.

Maybe now you have guessed the rest. They booked a holiday on the same cruise and, before the date, Mr Challinor has grown a big beard. On the voyage they act to make everyone know Mr Challinor with his beard. At the first opportunity they have stolen the cabin key of the victim – his name is Mr Andrew Pennyman – before they have killed him and thrown the body overboard. The details of who made the murder and how are not yet clear.

Immediately Mr Challinor went into the cabin of Mr Pennyman, shaved away his beard and stayed there all the voyage. The steward left his meals outside the cabin door and now and then Mrs Challinor brought to him extra things. At disembarkation Mr Challinor came out in Mr Pennyman's clothes and with Mr Pennyman's luggage.

Mr and Mrs Challinor stayed apart on the buses and on the aeroplane. Their one mistake – I have learned that every criminal always makes at least one mistake – was to take the same taxi from the airport to la Boca, from where leaves the ferry to Uruguay. You were in that spot to see them together.

Mr Pound, may I thank you again for help in all these events. I have asked the police to try to keep your name from the media, but so many are those involved I cannot promise this.

My regards.

Harken

So the coincidence, thought Harry, was just a small one. There are only so many basic sizes, builds and looks in the human race. Looking up and down the train he even saw one chap who on a dark night could pass for himself. For two to be in the same London pub at the same time is not that improbable. The chances of this happening when one of them could take advantage it are also not too high. Mystery solved.

His phone beeped again. Sami again.

Dear Mr Pound

Welcome back to England, land of history and especially historical tours. Perhaps my previous message has been lost in the ether, as you yourself call it. I apologise for bothering you when you must be very tired from your flight, but our telephone has been truly alive with calls from the newspapers asking for you and referring to an incident in South America. Now I have a young lady from the BBC parked outside the office awaiting your return. Please advise.

Yours sincerely,

S Khatri

Oh dear, thought Hieronymus Pound, watching the drizzle run down the train window. Spain is nice at this time of year.

Also by George Quin:

Murder in Minsk (2015)
Murder in Appledore (2019)

Murder in Minsk, *Murder in Appledore* and *Murder in Antarctica* are all available from Amazon.com and other retail outlets. As e-books, they are available on Kindle and other devices.

Printed in Great Britain
by Amazon